GEORGE O'CONNOR

HADES

LORD OF THE DEAD

A NEAL PORTER BOOK

First Second
New York & London

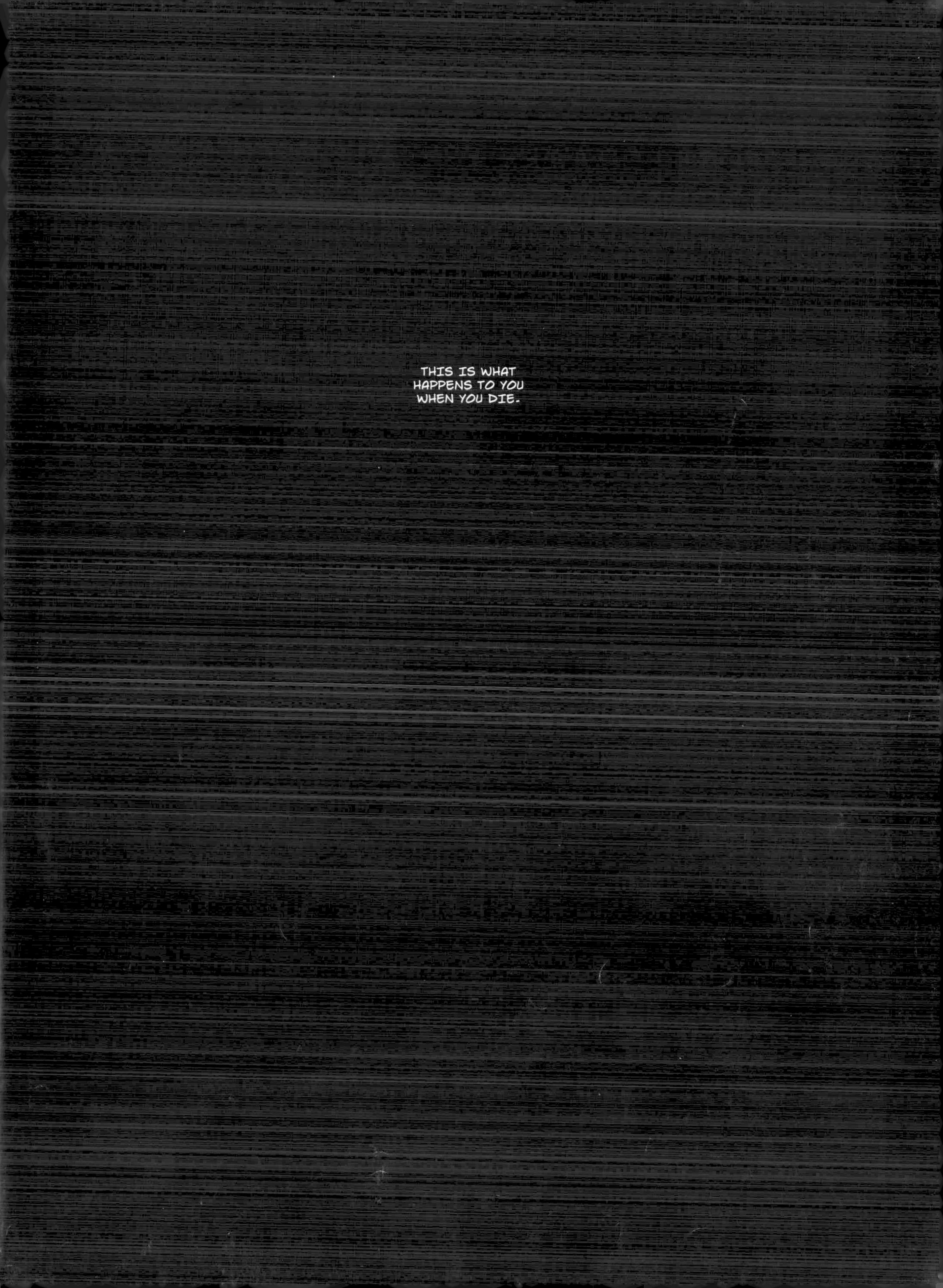
THIS IS WHAT HAPPENS TO YOU WHEN YOU DIE.

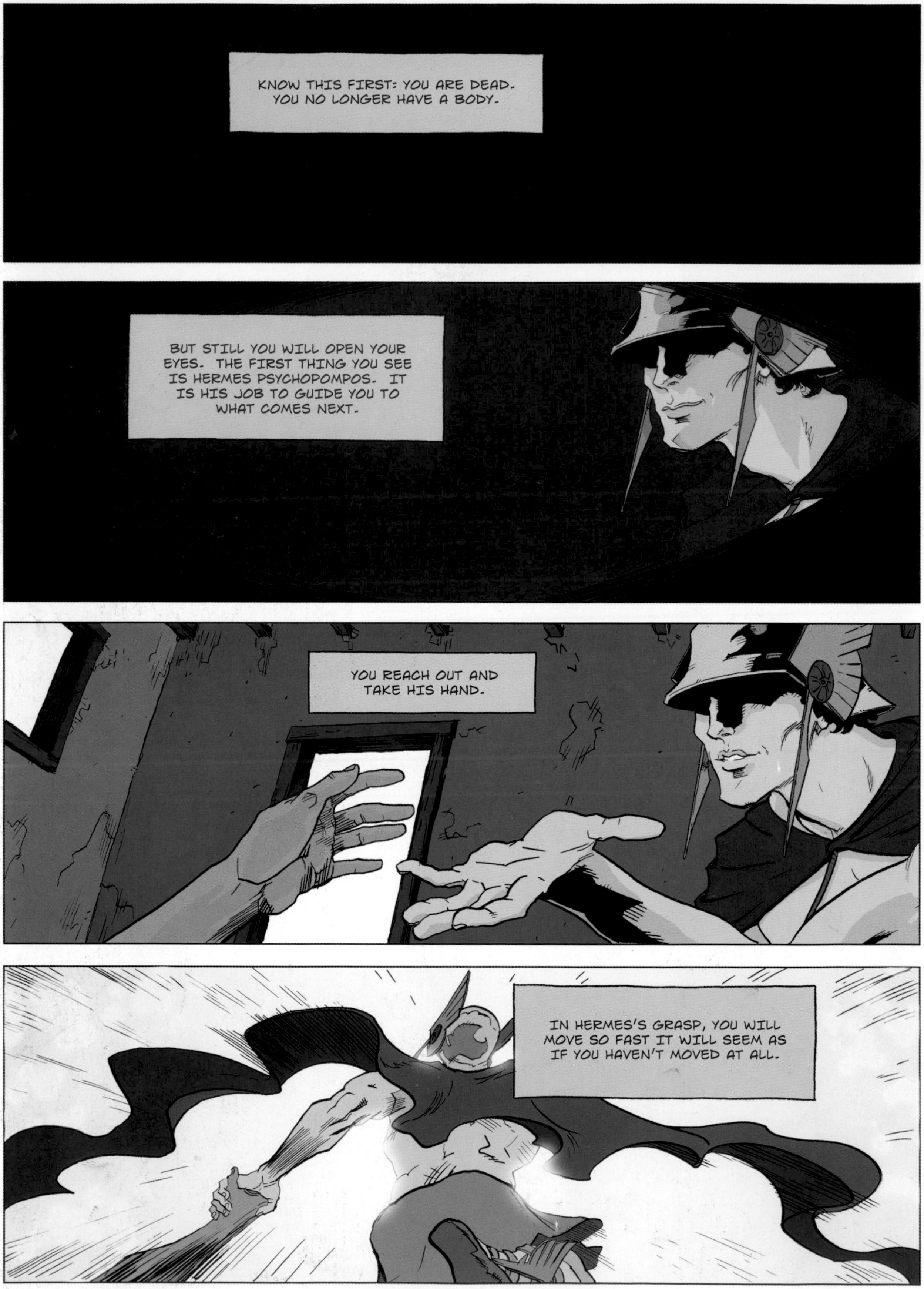
KNOW THIS FIRST: YOU ARE DEAD. YOU NO LONGER HAVE A BODY.
BUT STILL YOU WILL OPEN YOUR EYES. THE FIRST THING YOU SEE IS HERMES PSYCHOPOMPOS. IT IS HIS JOB TO GUIDE YOU TO WHAT COMES NEXT.
YOU REACH OUT AND TAKE HIS HAND.
IN HERMES'S GRASP, YOU WILL MOVE SO FAST IT WILL SEEM AS IF YOU HAVEN'T MOVED AT ALL.

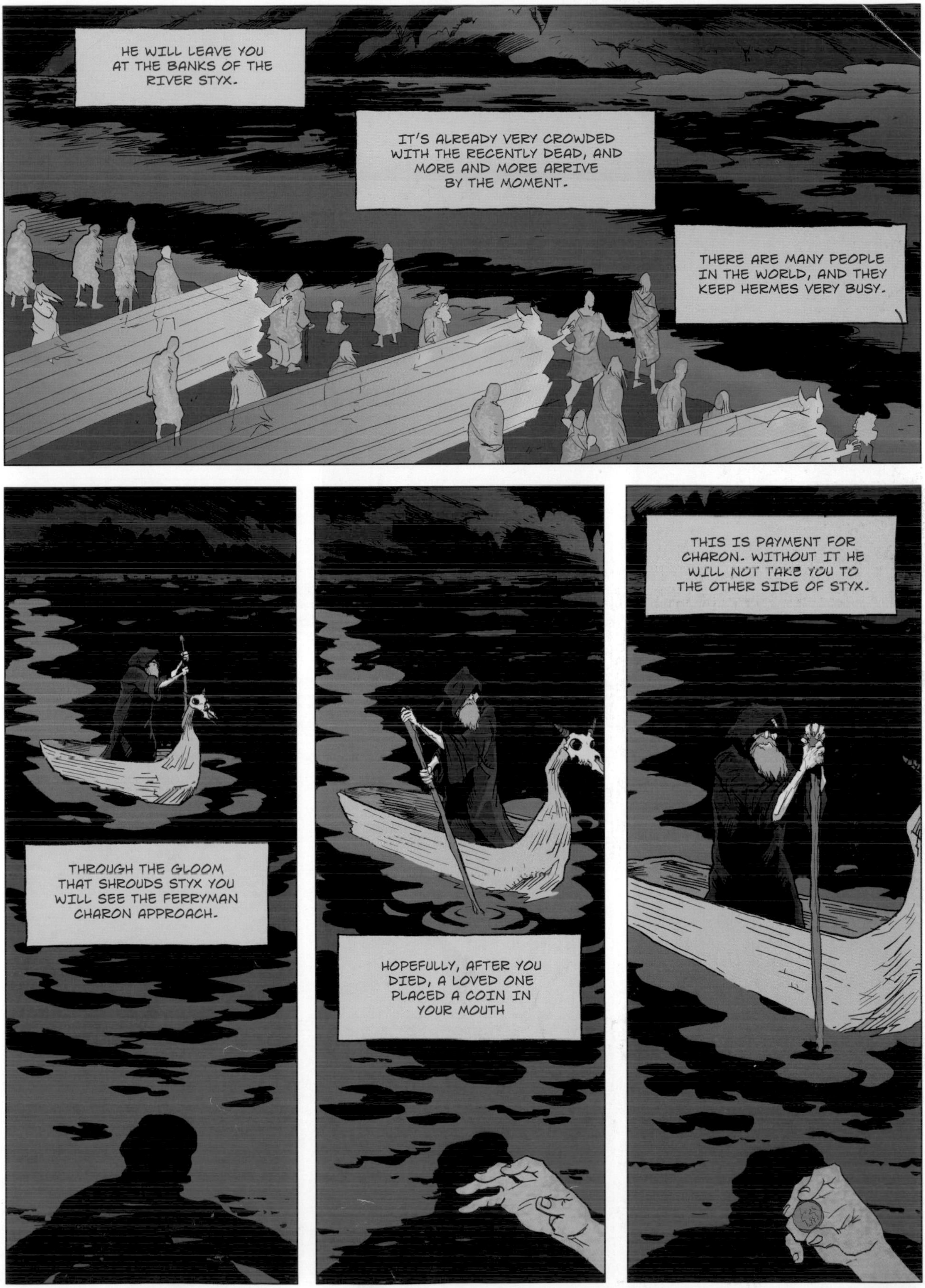
HE WILL LEAVE YOU AT THE BANKS OF THE RIVER STYX.
IT'S ALREADY VERY CROWDED WITH THE RECENTLY DEAD, AND MORE AND MORE ARRIVE BY THE MOMENT.
THERE ARE MANY PEOPLE IN THE WORLD, AND THEY KEEP HERMES VERY BUSY.
THROUGH THE GLOOM THAT SHROUDS STYX YOU WILL SEE THE FERRYMAN CHARON APPROACH.
HOPEFULLY, AFTER YOU DIED, A LOVED ONE PLACED A COIN IN YOUR MOUTH
THIS IS PAYMENT FOR CHARON. WITHOUT IT HE WILL NOT TAKE YOU TO THE OTHER SIDE OF STYX.

WITHOUT PAYMENT, YOU WOULD REMAIN FOR A HUNDRED YEARS ON THE CROWDED BANK OF STYX.

AFTER AN AGE OF TRAVEL, YOU WILL SEE CERBERUS, WHO GUARDS THE ENTRANCE TO THE UNDERWORLD.

HIS THREE HEADS WHIMPER A FRIENDLY GREETING, AS HIS SERPENT TAIL WAGS HELLO.

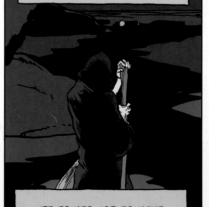

IT IS HIS JOB TO MAKE SURE THE DEAD DO NOT LEAVE THE UNDERWORLD. HE WOULD NOT BE SO FRIENDLY IF YOU WERE TO SEE HIM AGAIN.

ONCE YOU ARE PAST CERBERUS, THE FAR SHORE OF STYX COMES INTO VIEW.

AS CROWDED AS THE NEAR SHORE OF STYX WAS, THIS PLACE, CALLED EREBUS, IS EVEN MORE SO.

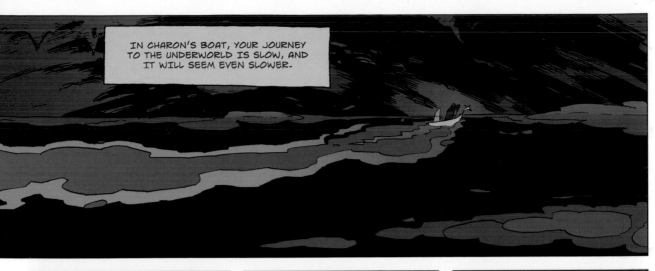

IN CHARON'S BOAT, YOUR JOURNEY TO THE UNDERWORLD IS SLOW, AND IT WILL SEEM EVEN SLOWER.

IF YOU STILL HAD A BODY, THE ANONYMOUS SHADES OF THE DEAD WOULD SURROUND YOU, DRAWN TO YOUR HOT BLOOD AND FLESH. THE DEAD MISS BEING ALIVE LIKE THE THIRSTY MISS WATER.

BUT YOU DON'T HAVE A BODY ANY MORE, SO THEY WILL NOT EVEN NOTICE YOUR PASSING.

HERE AND THERE, AMONGST THE CROWD, A SHADE IS SET APART FROM THE REST.

A WOMAN, CURSED IN LIFE BY THE GODS, MOVES THROUGH THE CROWD, SCATTERING THE FRIGHTENED DEAD BEFORE HER. FROM BENEATH HER HOOD, HER HAIR OF SNAKES POKES OUT AND TASTES THE STILL AIR.

OVER THERE, THE MORTAL HALF OF HERACLES STANDS, WONDERING AFTER HIS DIVINE HALF, AND STARES AT MOUNT OLYMPUS, OR WHERE HE IMAGINES OLYMPUS TO BE.

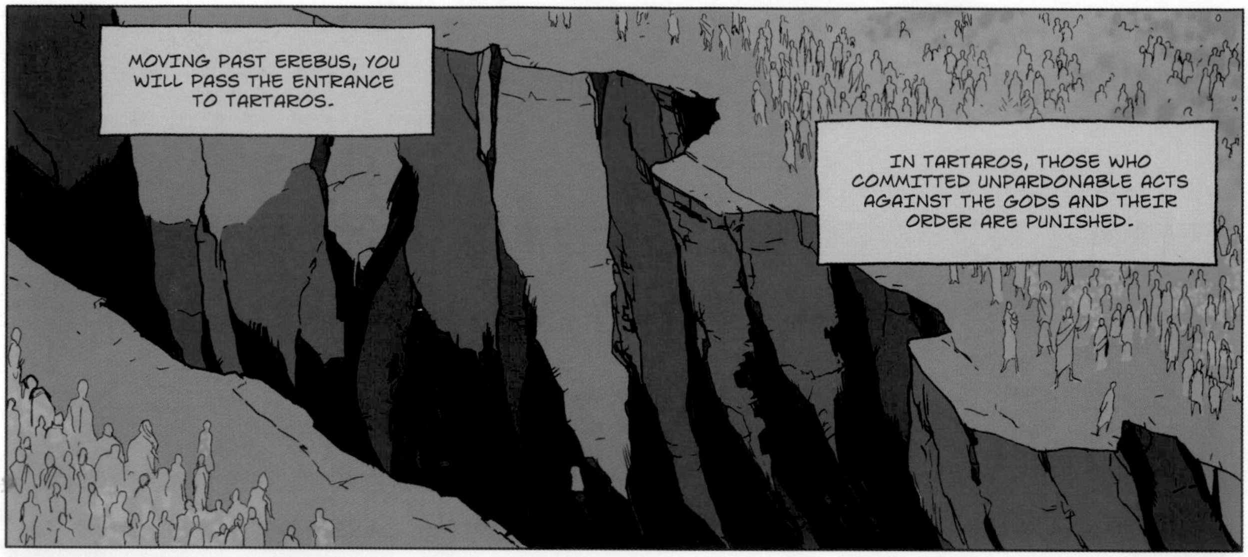
MOVING PAST EREBUS, YOU WILL PASS THE ENTRANCE TO TARTAROS.
IN TARTAROS, THOSE WHO COMMITTED UNPARDONABLE ACTS AGAINST THE GODS AND THEIR ORDER ARE PUNISHED.

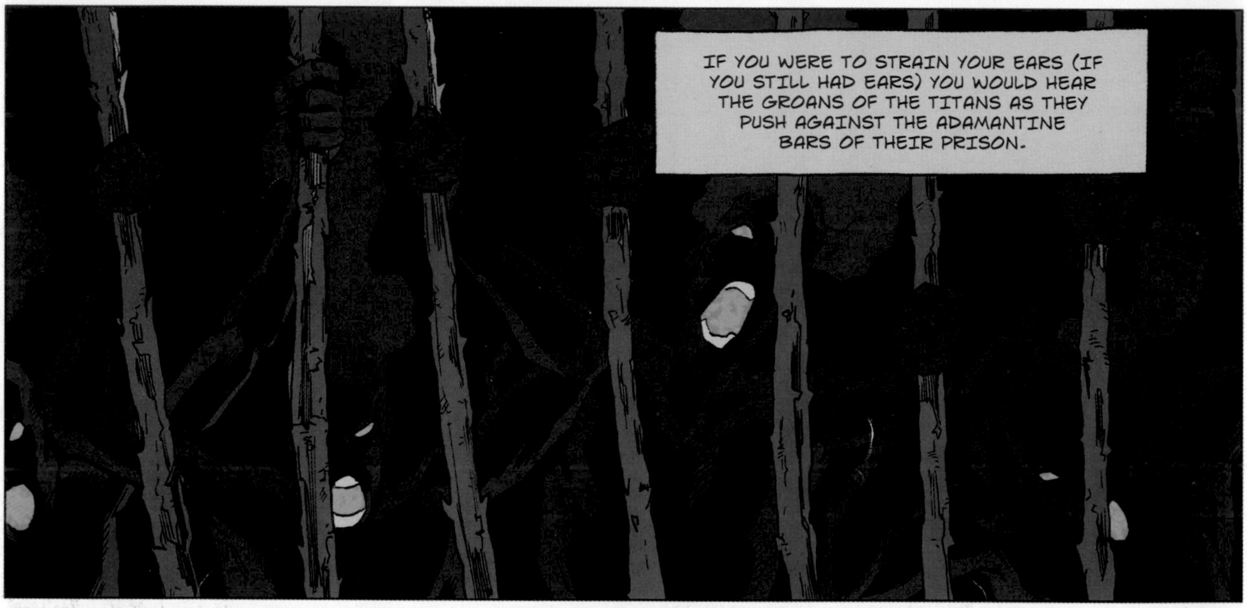
IF YOU WERE TO STRAIN YOUR EARS (IF YOU STILL HAD EARS) YOU WOULD HEAR THE GROANS OF THE TITANS AS THEY PUSH AGAINST THE ADAMANTINE BARS OF THEIR PRISON.

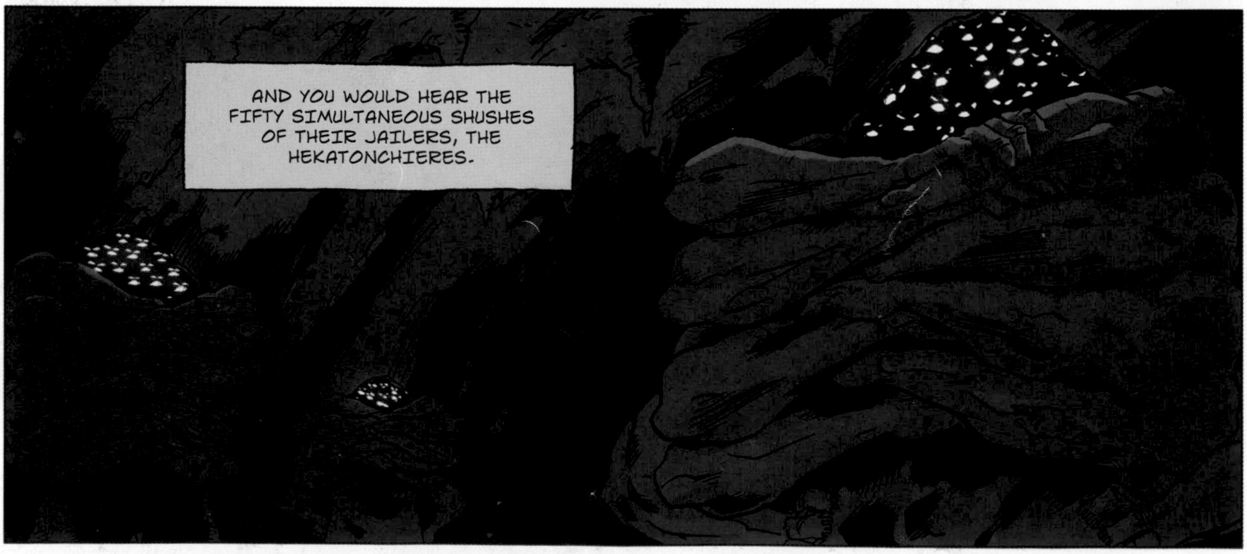
AND YOU WOULD HEAR THE FIFTY SIMULTANEOUS SHUSHES OF THEIR JAILERS, THE HEKATONCHIERES.

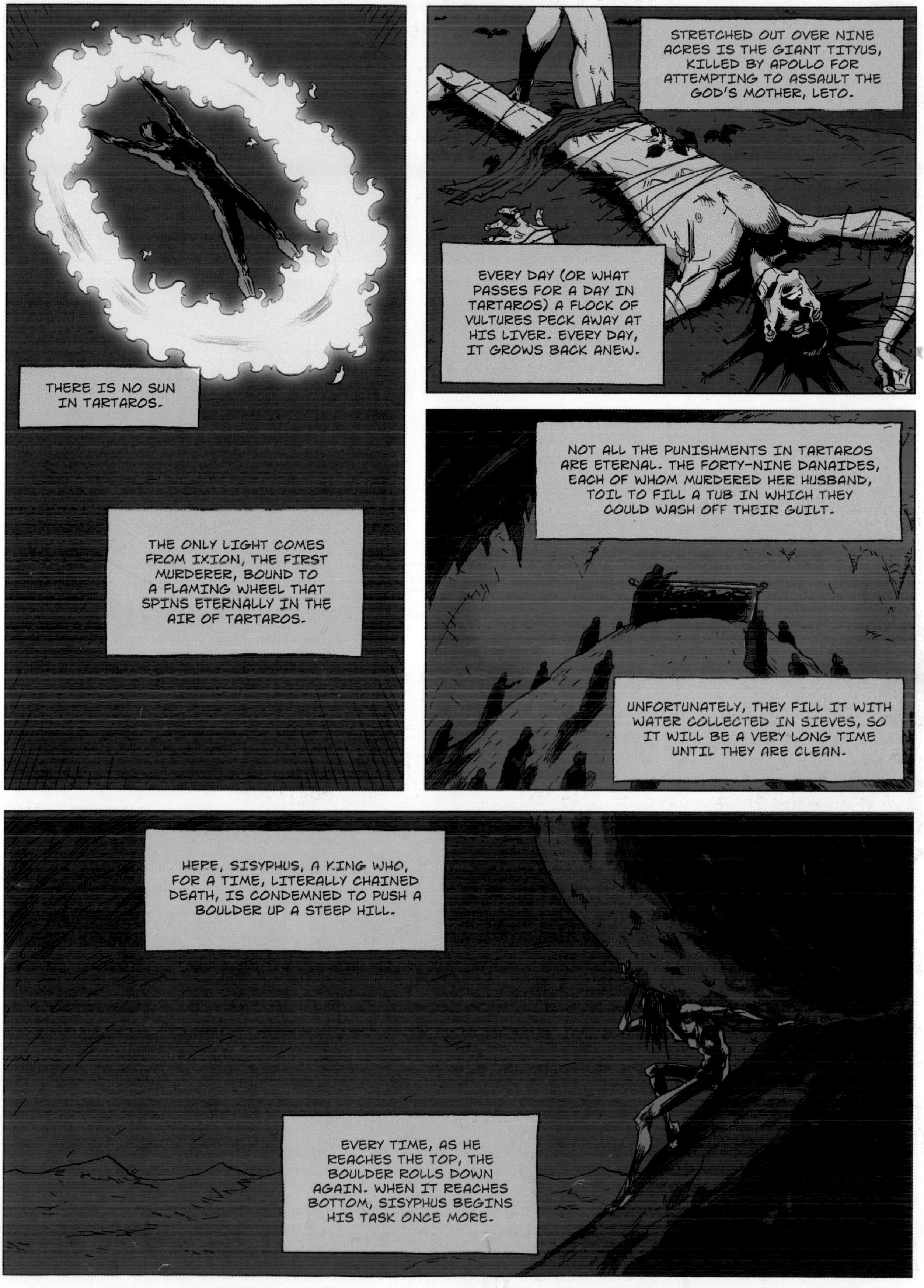
THERE IS NO SUN IN TARTAROS.
THE ONLY LIGHT COMES FROM IXION, THE FIRST MURDERER, BOUND TO A FLAMING WHEEL THAT SPINS ETERNALLY IN THE AIR OF TARTAROS.
STRETCHED OUT OVER NINE ACRES IS THE GIANT TITYUS, KILLED BY APOLLO FOR ATTEMPTING TO ASSAULT THE GOD'S MOTHER, LETO.
EVERY DAY (OR WHAT PASSES FOR A DAY IN TARTAROS) A FLOCK OF VULTURES PECK AWAY AT HIS LIVER. EVERY DAY, IT GROWS BACK ANEW.
NOT ALL THE PUNISHMENTS IN TARTAROS ARE ETERNAL. THE FORTY-NINE DANAIDES, EACH OF WHOM MURDERED HER HUSBAND, TOIL TO FILL A TUB IN WHICH THEY COULD WASH OFF THEIR GUILT.
UNFORTUNATELY, THEY FILL IT WITH WATER COLLECTED IN SIEVES, SO IT WILL BE A VERY LONG TIME UNTIL THEY ARE CLEAN.
HERE, SISYPHUS, A KING WHO, FOR A TIME, LITERALLY CHAINED DEATH, IS CONDEMNED TO PUSH A BOULDER UP A STEEP HILL.
EVERY TIME, AS HE REACHES THE TOP, THE BOULDER ROLLS DOWN AGAIN. WHEN IT REACHES BOTTOM, SISYPHUS BEGINS HIS TASK ONCE MORE.

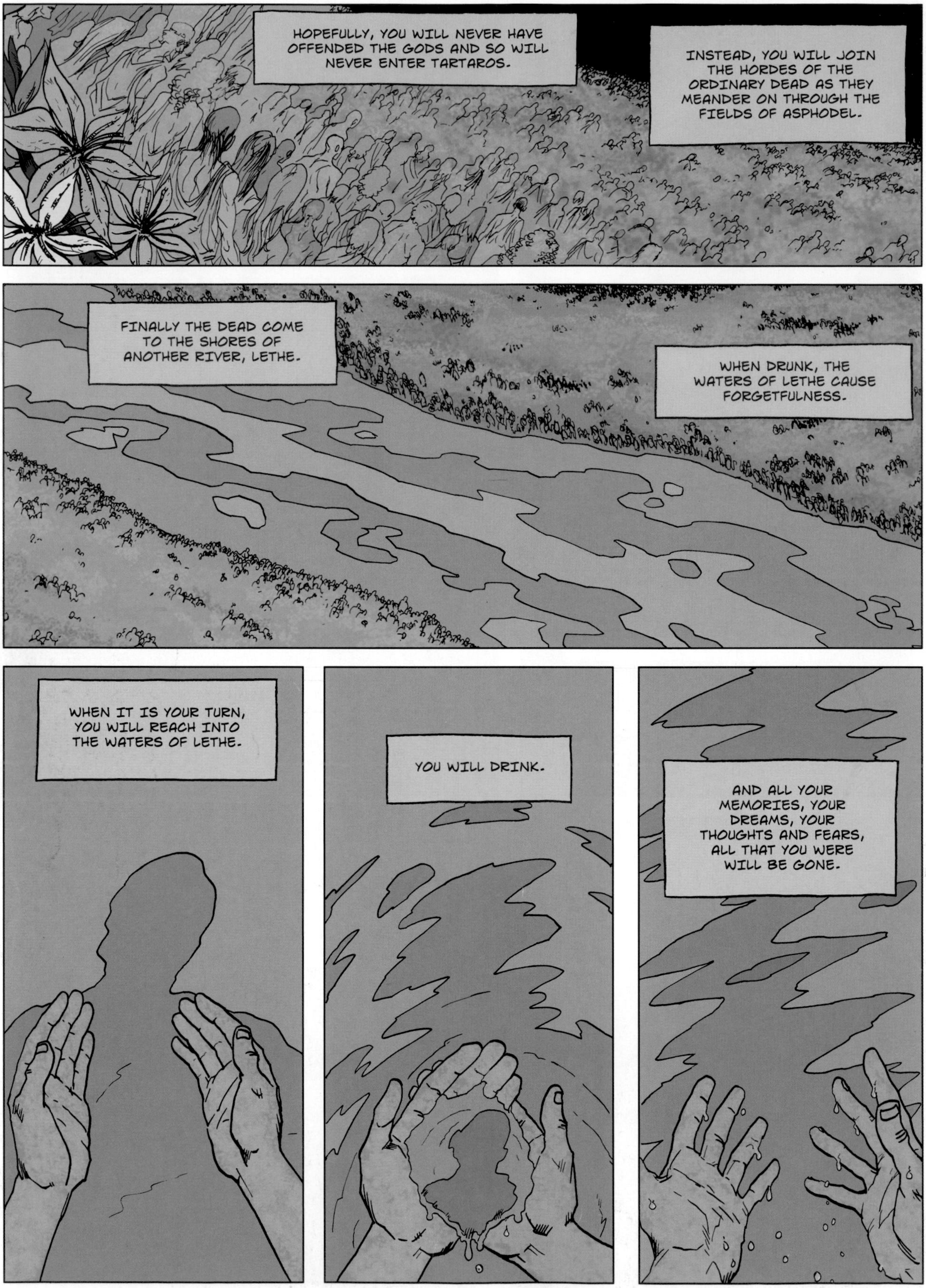
HOPEFULLY, YOU WILL NEVER HAVE OFFENDED THE GODS AND SO WILL NEVER ENTER TARTAROS.
INSTEAD, YOU WILL JOIN THE HORDES OF THE ORDINARY DEAD AS THEY MEANDER ON THROUGH THE FIELDS OF ASPHODEL.
FINALLY THE DEAD COME TO THE SHORES OF ANOTHER RIVER, LETHE.
WHEN DRUNK, THE WATERS OF LETHE CAUSE FORGETFULNESS.
WHEN IT IS YOUR TURN, YOU WILL REACH INTO THE WATERS OF LETHE.
YOU WILL DRINK.
AND ALL YOUR MEMORIES, YOUR DREAMS, YOUR THOUGHTS AND FEARS, ALL THAT YOU WERE WILL BE GONE.

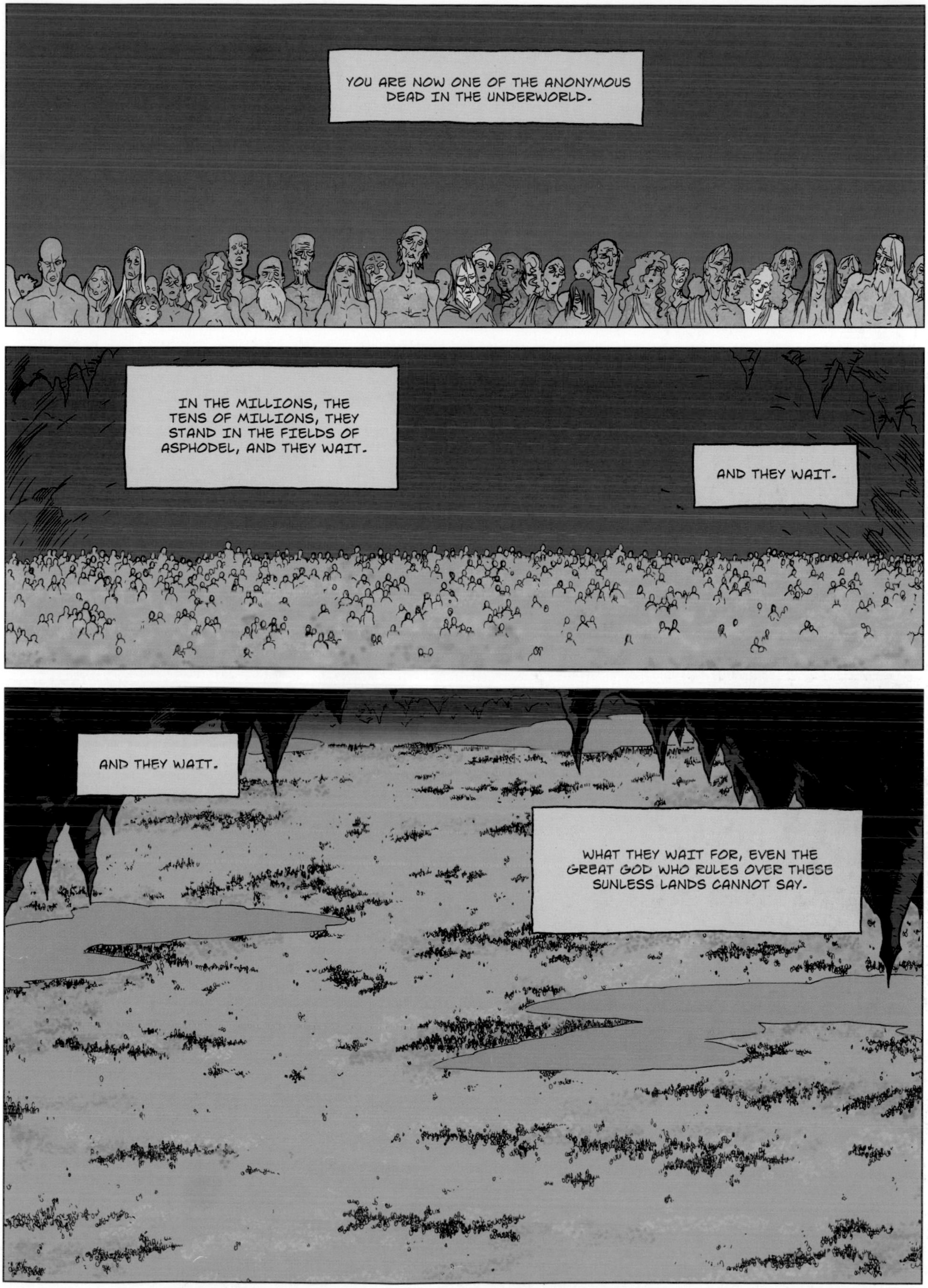

YOU ARE NOW ONE OF THE ANONYMOUS DEAD IN THE UNDERWORLD.
IN THE MILLIONS, THE TENS OF MILLIONS, THEY STAND IN THE FIELDS OF ASPHODEL, AND THEY WAIT.
AND THEY WAIT.
AND THEY WAIT.
WHAT THEY WAIT FOR, EVEN THE GREAT GOD WHO RULES OVER THESE SUNLESS LANDS CANNOT SAY.

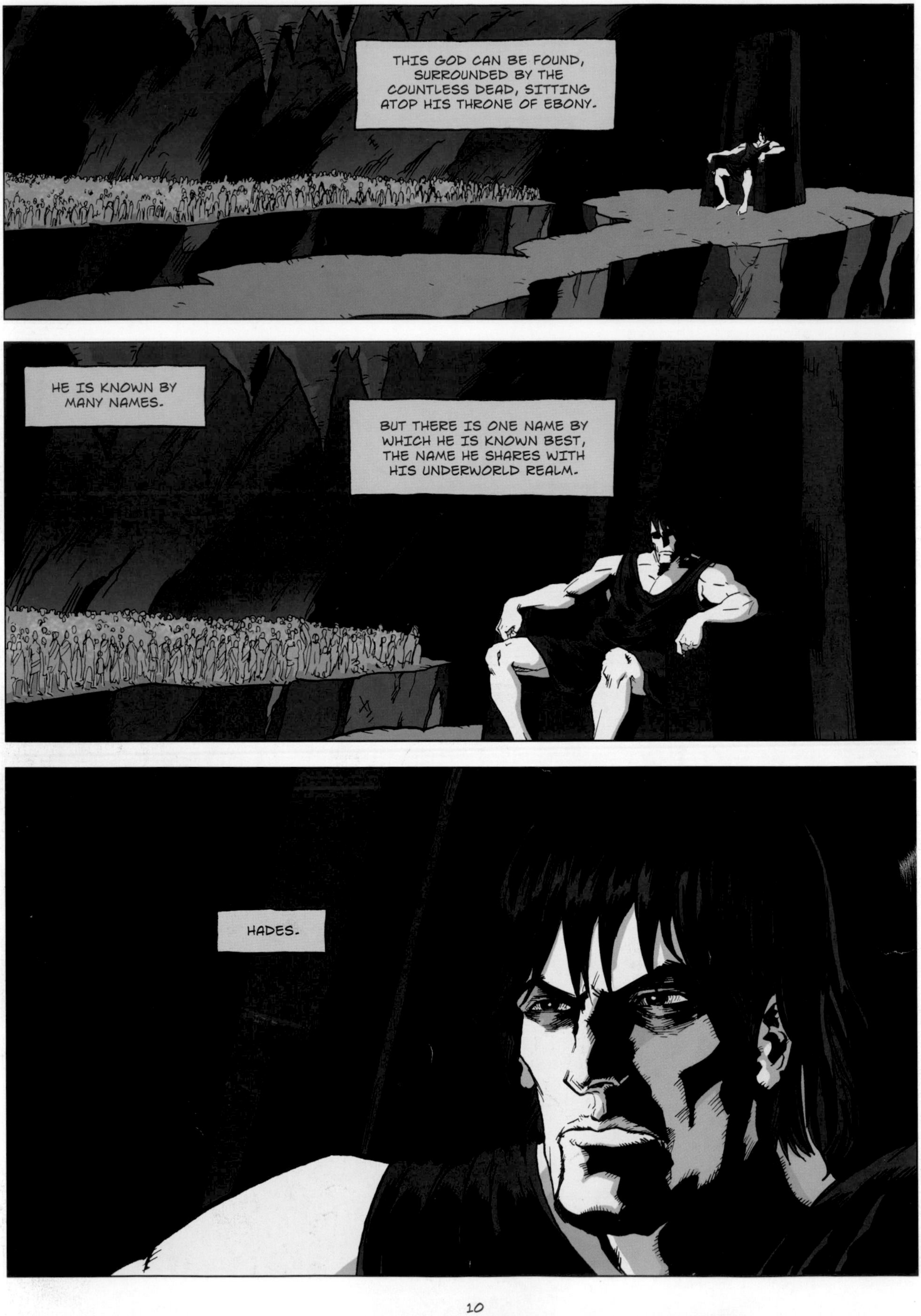
THIS GOD CAN BE FOUND, SURROUNDED BY THE COUNTLESS DEAD, SITTING ATOP HIS THRONE OF EBONY.
HE IS KNOWN BY MANY NAMES.
BUT THERE IS ONE NAME BY WHICH HE IS KNOWN BEST, THE NAME HE SHARES WITH HIS UNDERWORLD REALM.
HADES.

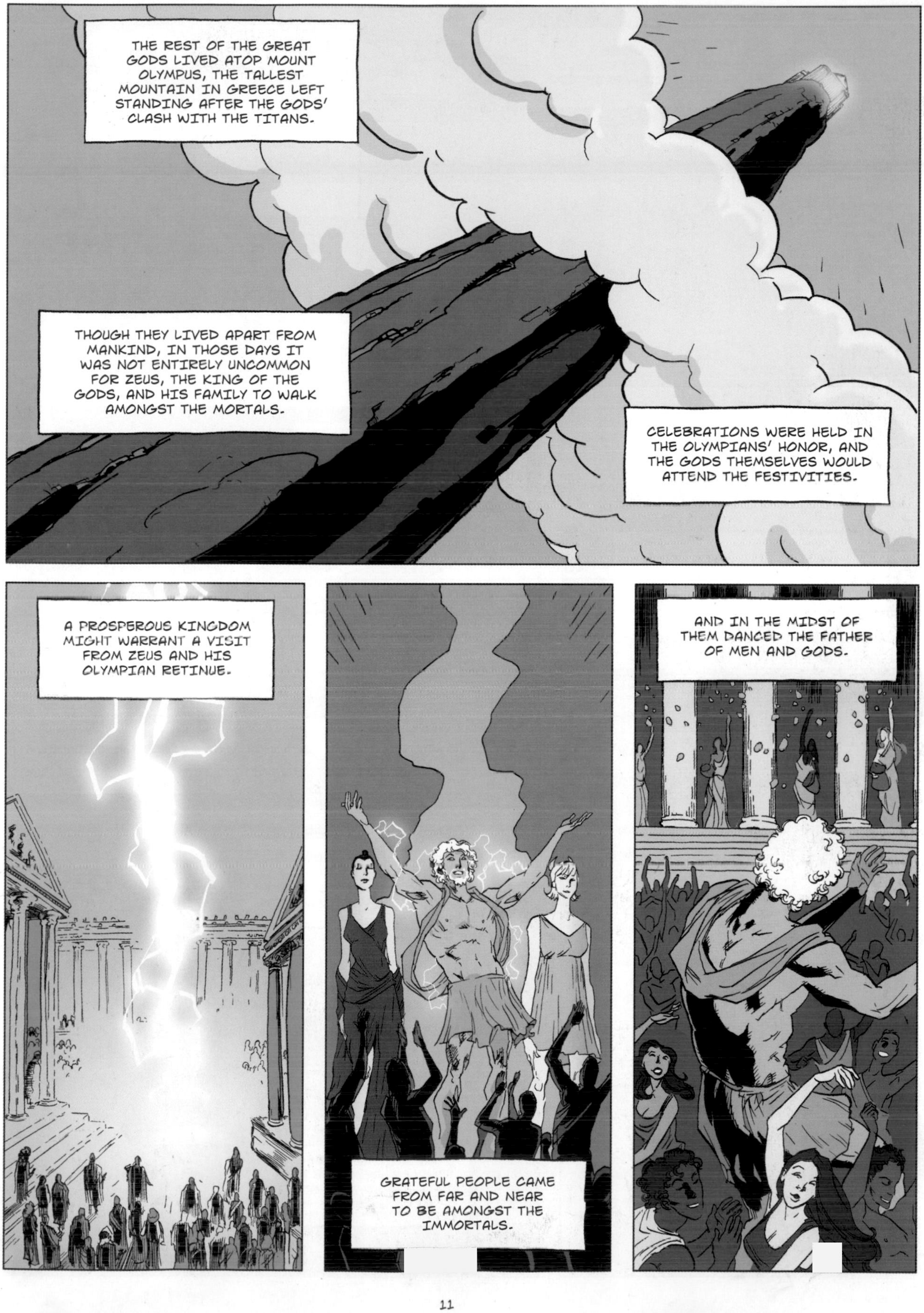
THE REST OF THE GREAT GODS LIVED ATOP MOUNT OLYMPUS, THE TALLEST MOUNTAIN IN GREECE LEFT STANDING AFTER THE GODS' CLASH WITH THE TITANS.
THOUGH THEY LIVED APART FROM MANKIND, IN THOSE DAYS IT WAS NOT ENTIRELY UNCOMMON FOR ZEUS, THE KING OF THE GODS, AND HIS FAMILY TO WALK AMONGST THE MORTALS.
CELEBRATIONS WERE HELD IN THE OLYMPIANS' HONOR, AND THE GODS THEMSELVES WOULD ATTEND THE FESTIVITIES.
A PROSPEROUS KINGDOM MIGHT WARRANT A VISIT FROM ZEUS AND HIS OLYMPIAN RETINUE.
GRATEFUL PEOPLE CAME FROM FAR AND NEAR TO BE AMONGST THE IMMORTALS.
AND IN THE MIDST OF THEM DANCED THE FATHER OF MEN AND GODS.

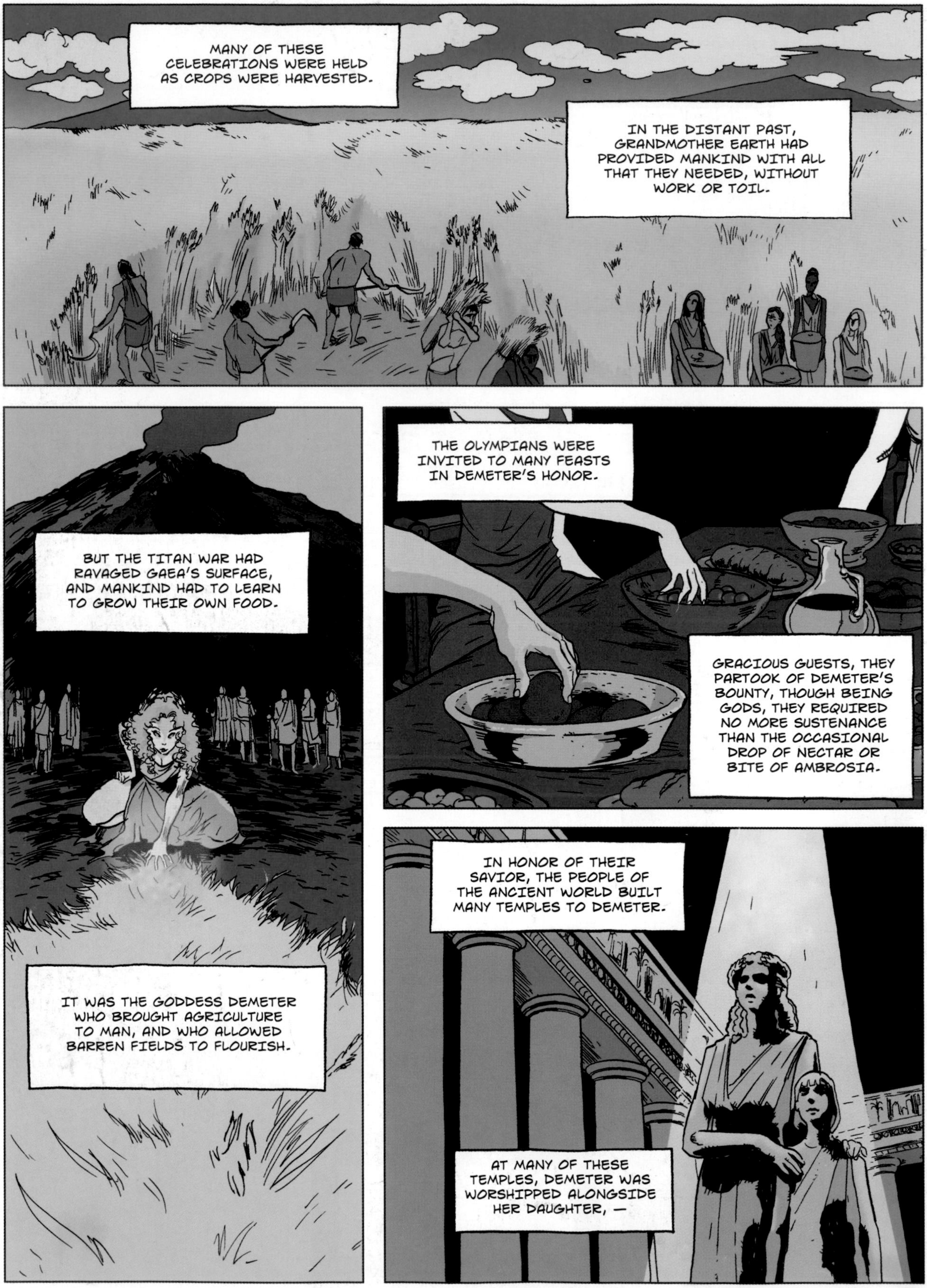
MANY OF THESE CELEBRATIONS WERE HELD AS CROPS WERE HARVESTED.
IN THE DISTANT PAST, GRANDMOTHER EARTH HAD PROVIDED MANKIND WITH ALL THAT THEY NEEDED, WITHOUT WORK OR TOIL.
BUT THE TITAN WAR HAD RAVAGED GAEA'S SURFACE, AND MANKIND HAD TO LEARN TO GROW THEIR OWN FOOD.
IT WAS THE GODDESS DEMETER WHO BROUGHT AGRICULTURE TO MAN, AND WHO ALLOWED BARREN FIELDS TO FLOURISH.
THE OLYMPIANS WERE INVITED TO MANY FEASTS IN DEMETER'S HONOR.
GRACIOUS GUESTS, THEY PARTOOK OF DEMETER'S BOUNTY, THOUGH BEING GODS, THEY REQUIRED NO MORE SUSTENANCE THAN THE OCCASIONAL DROP OF NECTAR OR BITE OF AMBROSIA.
IN HONOR OF THEIR SAVIOR, THE PEOPLE OF THE ANCIENT WORLD BUILT MANY TEMPLES TO DEMETER.
AT MANY OF THESE TEMPLES, DEMETER WAS WORSHIPPED ALONGSIDE HER DAUGHTER, —

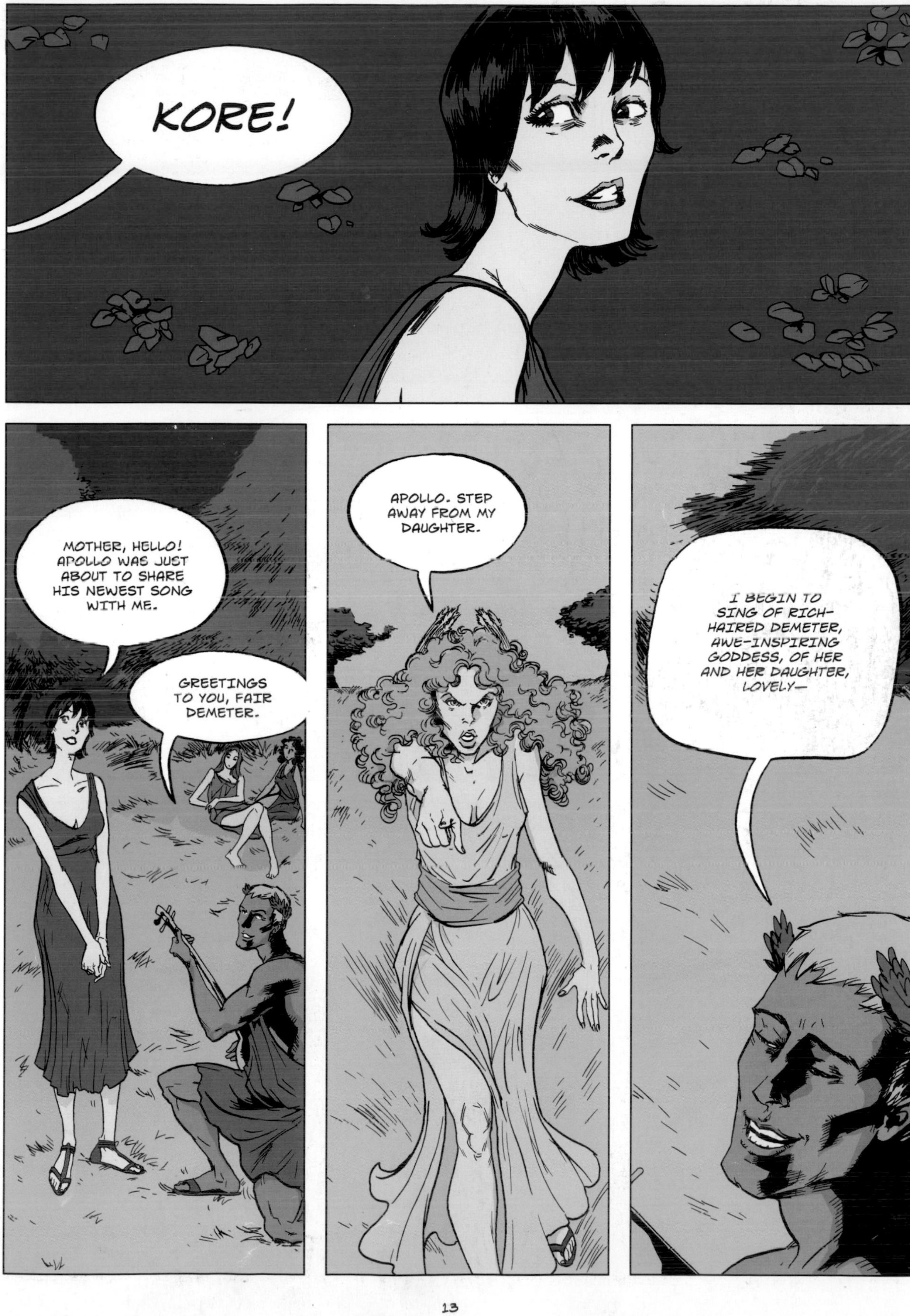
KORE!
MOTHER, HELLO! APOLLO WAS JUST ABOUT TO SHARE HIS NEWEST SONG WITH ME.
GREETINGS TO YOU, FAIR DEMETER.
APOLLO. STEP AWAY FROM MY DAUGHTER.
I BEGIN TO SING OF RICH-HAIRED DEMETER, AWE-INSPIRING GODDESS, OF HER AND HER DAUGHTER, LOVELY—

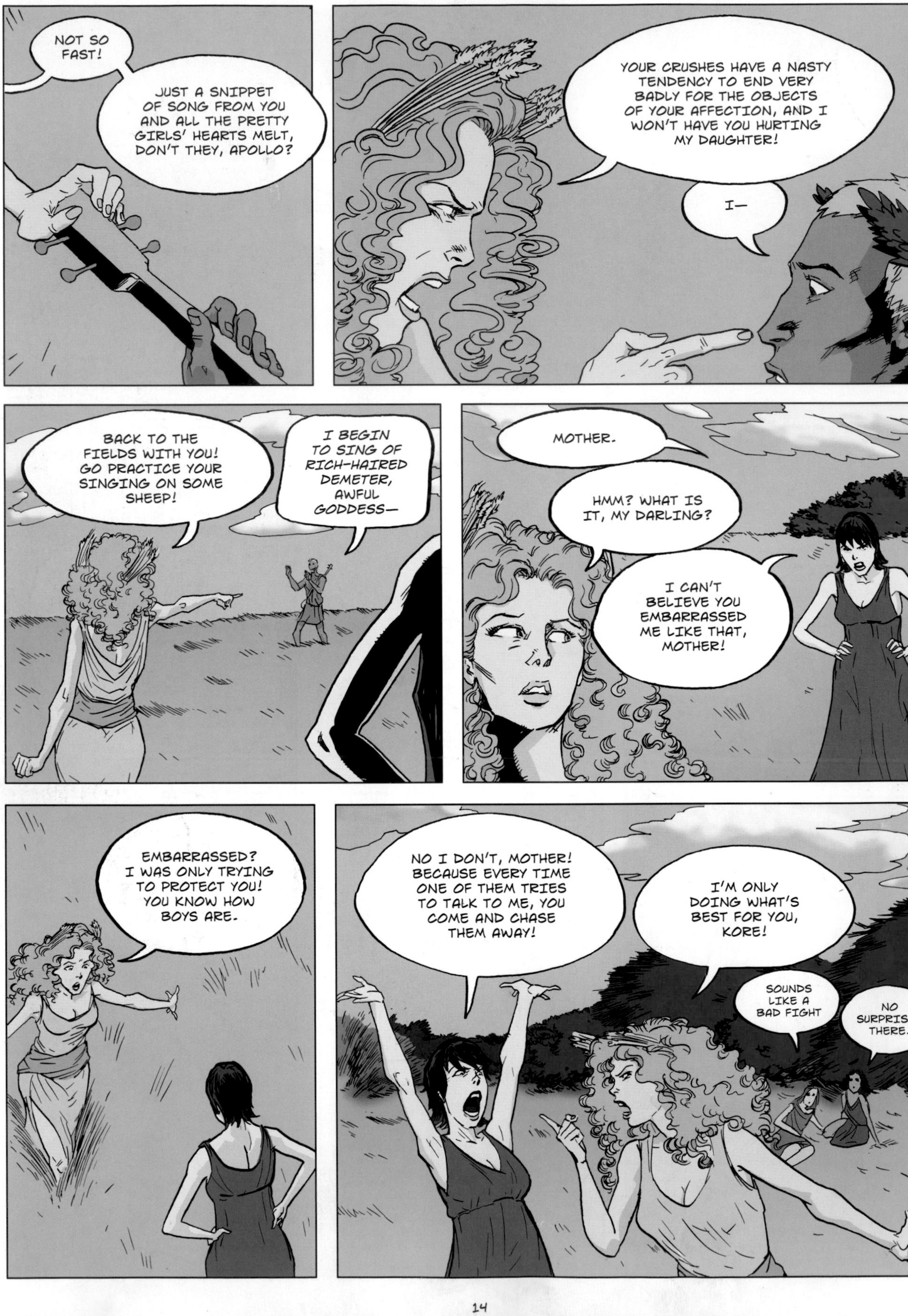
NOT SO FAST!
JUST A SNIPPET OF SONG FROM YOU AND ALL THE PRETTY GIRLS' HEARTS MELT, DON'T THEY, APOLLO?
YOUR CRUSHES HAVE A NASTY TENDENCY TO END VERY BADLY FOR THE OBJECTS OF YOUR AFFECTION, AND I WON'T HAVE YOU HURTING MY DAUGHTER!
I—
BACK TO THE FIELDS WITH YOU! GO PRACTICE YOUR SINGING ON SOME SHEEP!
I BEGIN TO SING OF RICH-HAIRED DEMETER, AWFUL GODDESS—
MOTHER.
HMM? WHAT IS IT, MY DARLING?
I CAN'T BELIEVE YOU EMBARRASSED ME LIKE THAT, MOTHER!
EMBARRASSED? I WAS ONLY TRYING TO PROTECT YOU! YOU KNOW HOW BOYS ARE.
NO I DON'T, MOTHER! BECAUSE EVERY TIME ONE OF THEM TRIES TO TALK TO ME, YOU COME AND CHASE THEM AWAY!
I'M ONLY DOING WHAT'S BEST FOR YOU, KORE!
SOUNDS LIKE A BAD FIGHT
NO SURPRISES THERE.

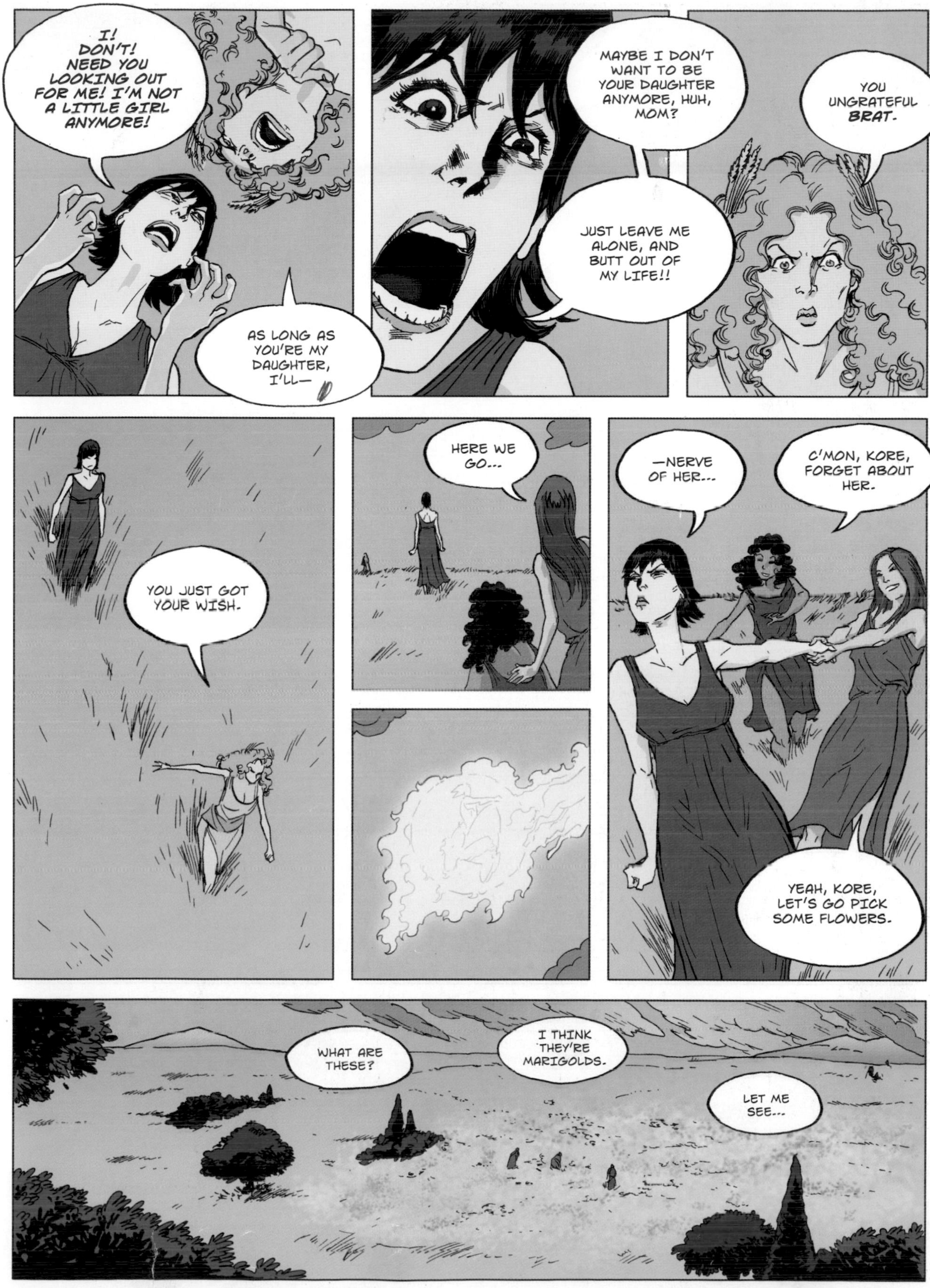
I! DON'T! NEED YOU LOOKING OUT FOR ME! I'M NOT A LITTLE GIRL ANYMORE!
AS LONG AS YOU'RE MY DAUGHTER, I'LL—
MAYBE I DON'T WANT TO BE YOUR DAUGHTER ANYMORE, HUH, MOM?
JUST LEAVE ME ALONE, AND BUTT OUT OF MY LIFE!!
YOU UNGRATEFUL BRAT.
YOU JUST GOT YOUR WISH.
HERE WE GO...
—NERVE OF HER...
C'MON, KORE, FORGET ABOUT HER.
YEAH, KORE, LET'S GO PICK SOME FLOWERS.
WHAT ARE THESE?
I THINK THEY'RE MARIGOLDS.
LET ME SEE...

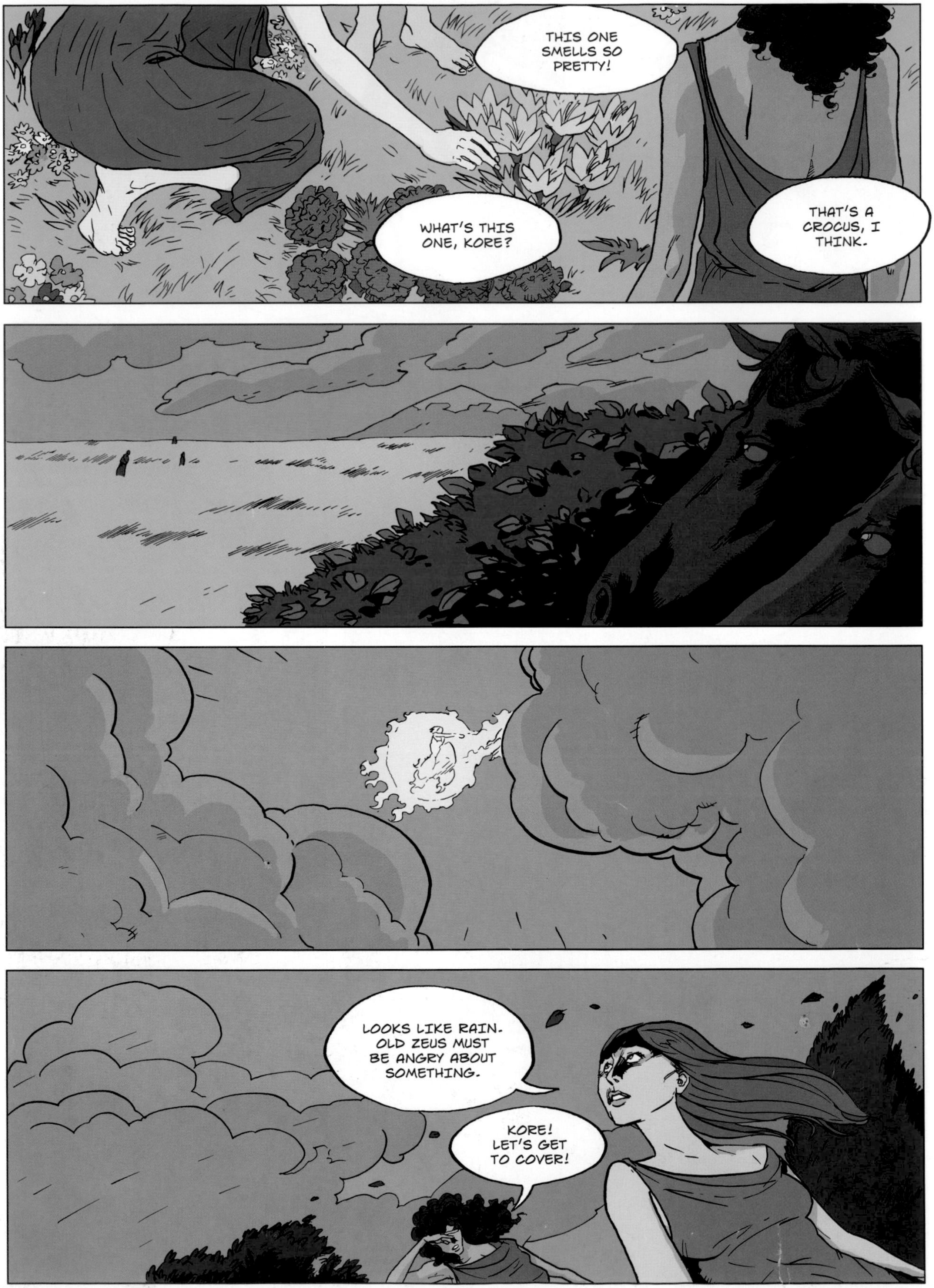
THIS ONE SMELLS SO PRETTY!
WHAT'S THIS ONE, KORE?
THAT'S A CROCUS, I THINK.
LOOKS LIKE RAIN. OLD ZEUS MUST BE ANGRY ABOUT SOMETHING.
KORE! LET'S GET TO COVER!

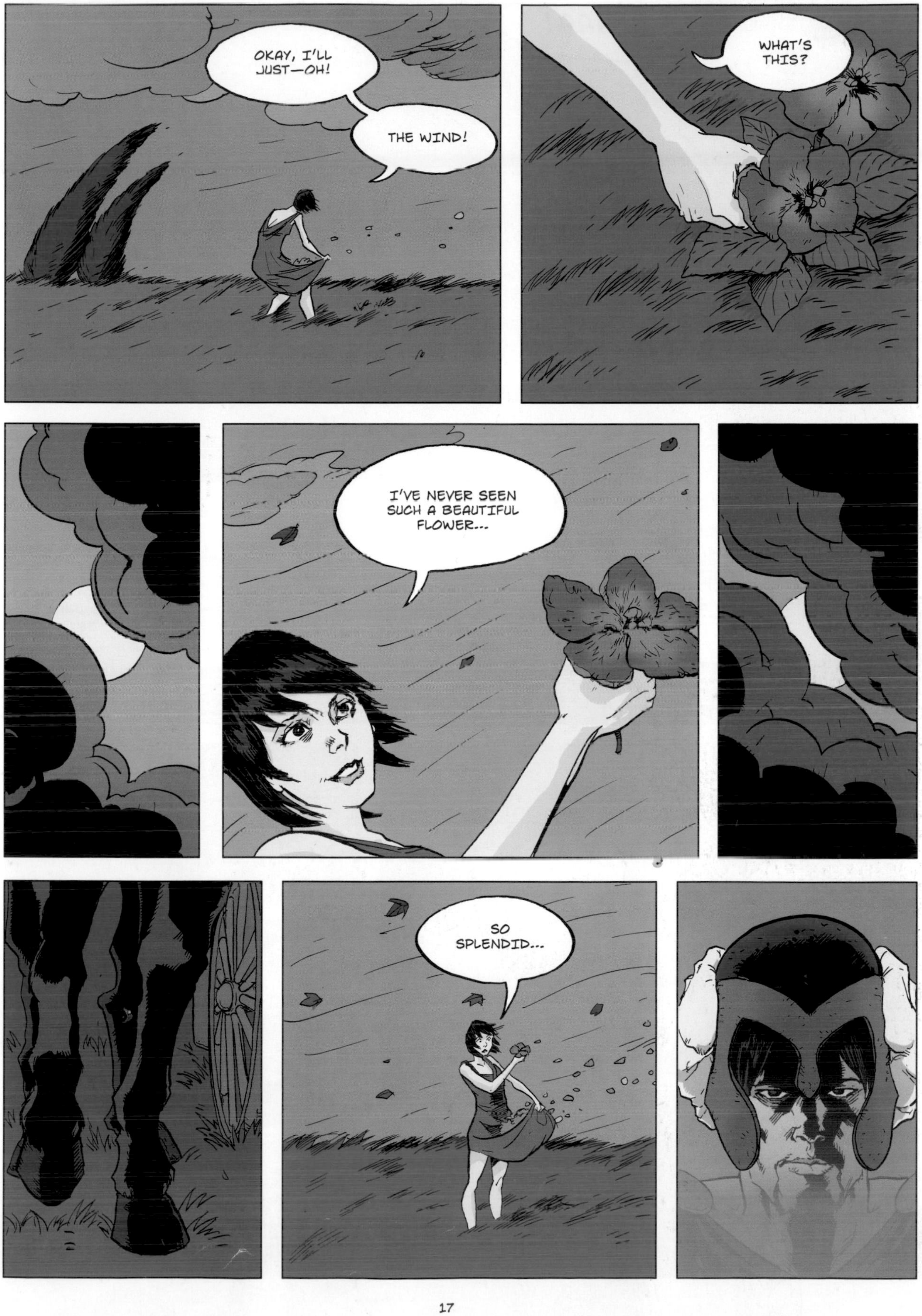
OKAY, I'LL JUST—OH!
THE WIND!
WHAT'S THIS?
I'VE NEVER SEEN SUCH A BEAUTIFUL FLOWER...
SO SPLENDID...

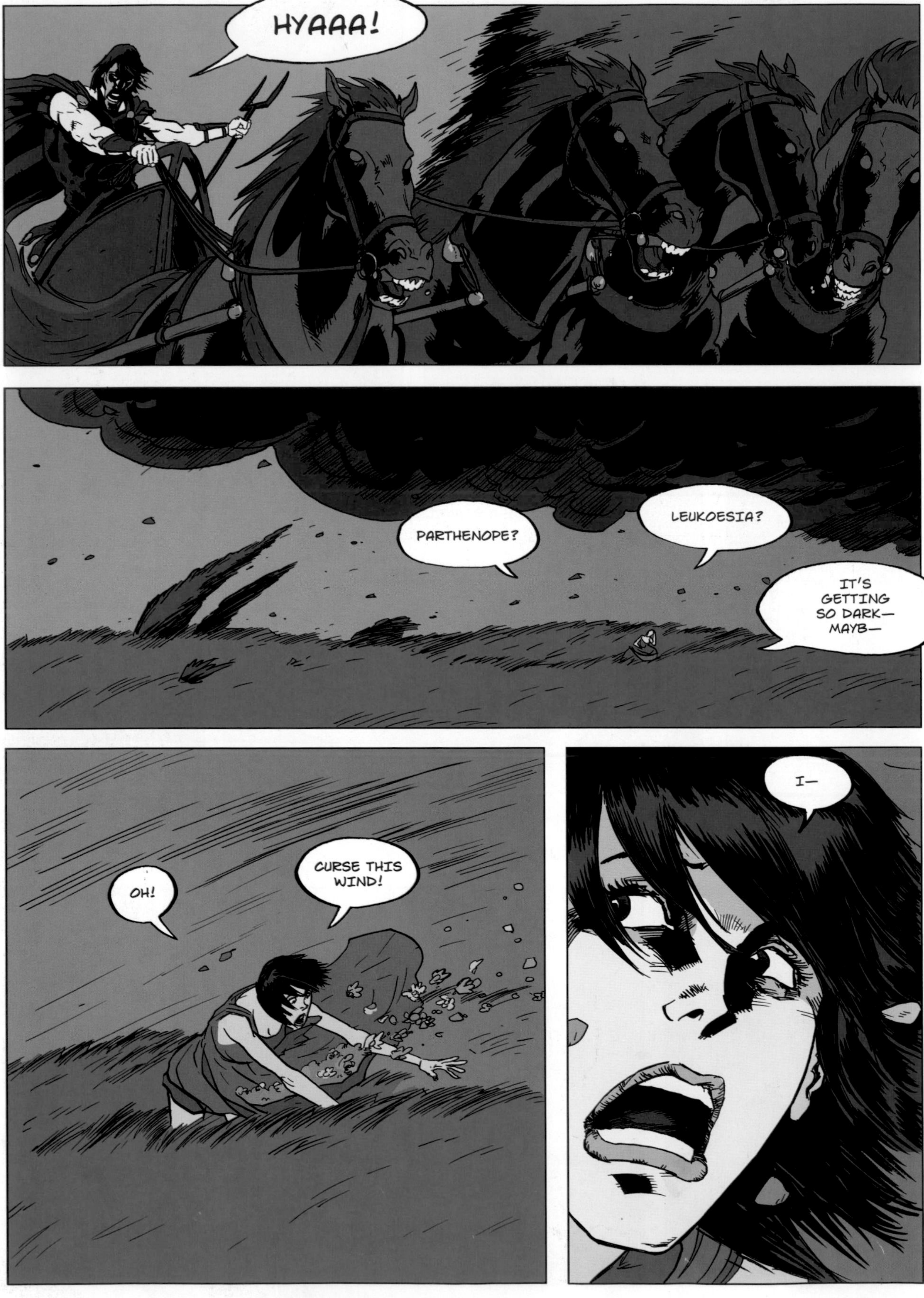
HYAAA!
PARTHENOPE?
LEUKOESIA?
IT'S GETTING SO DARK— MAYB—
OH!
CURSE THIS WIND!
I—

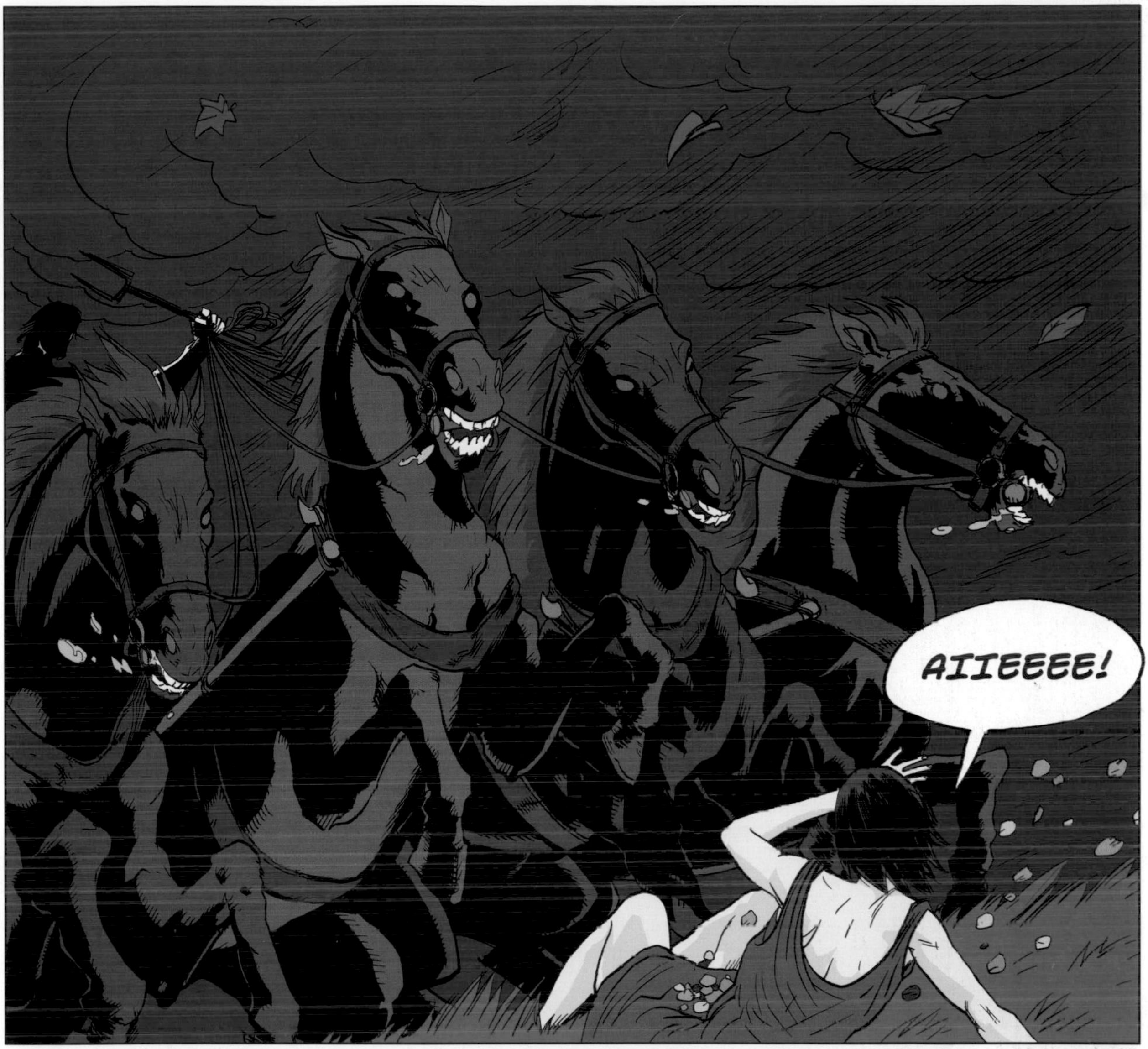
AIIEEEE!

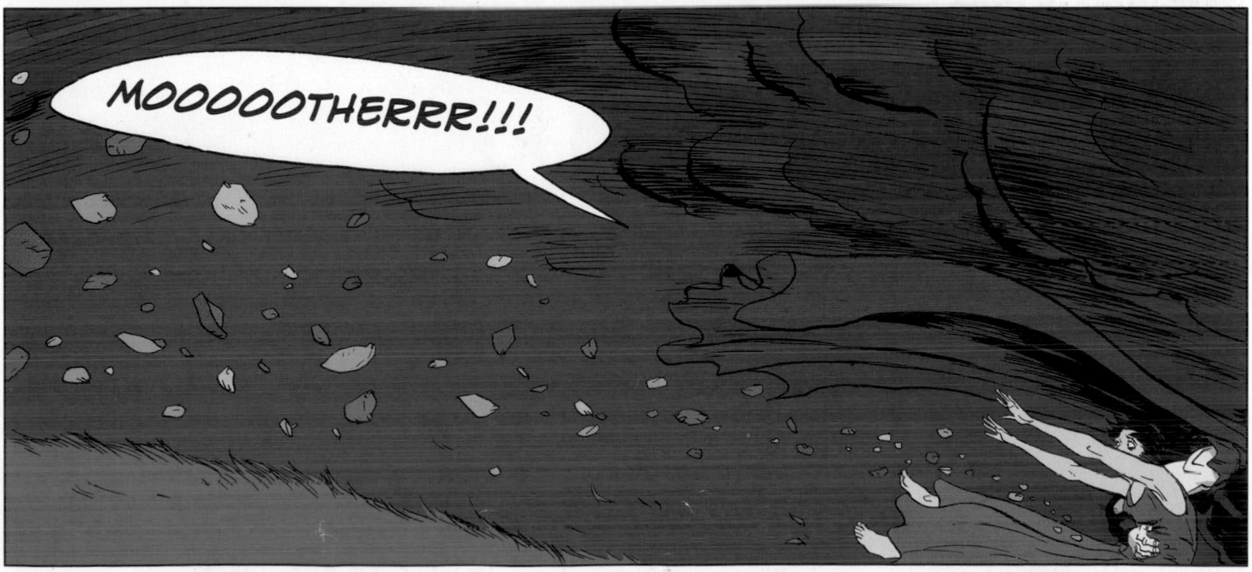
MOOOOOTHERRR!!!

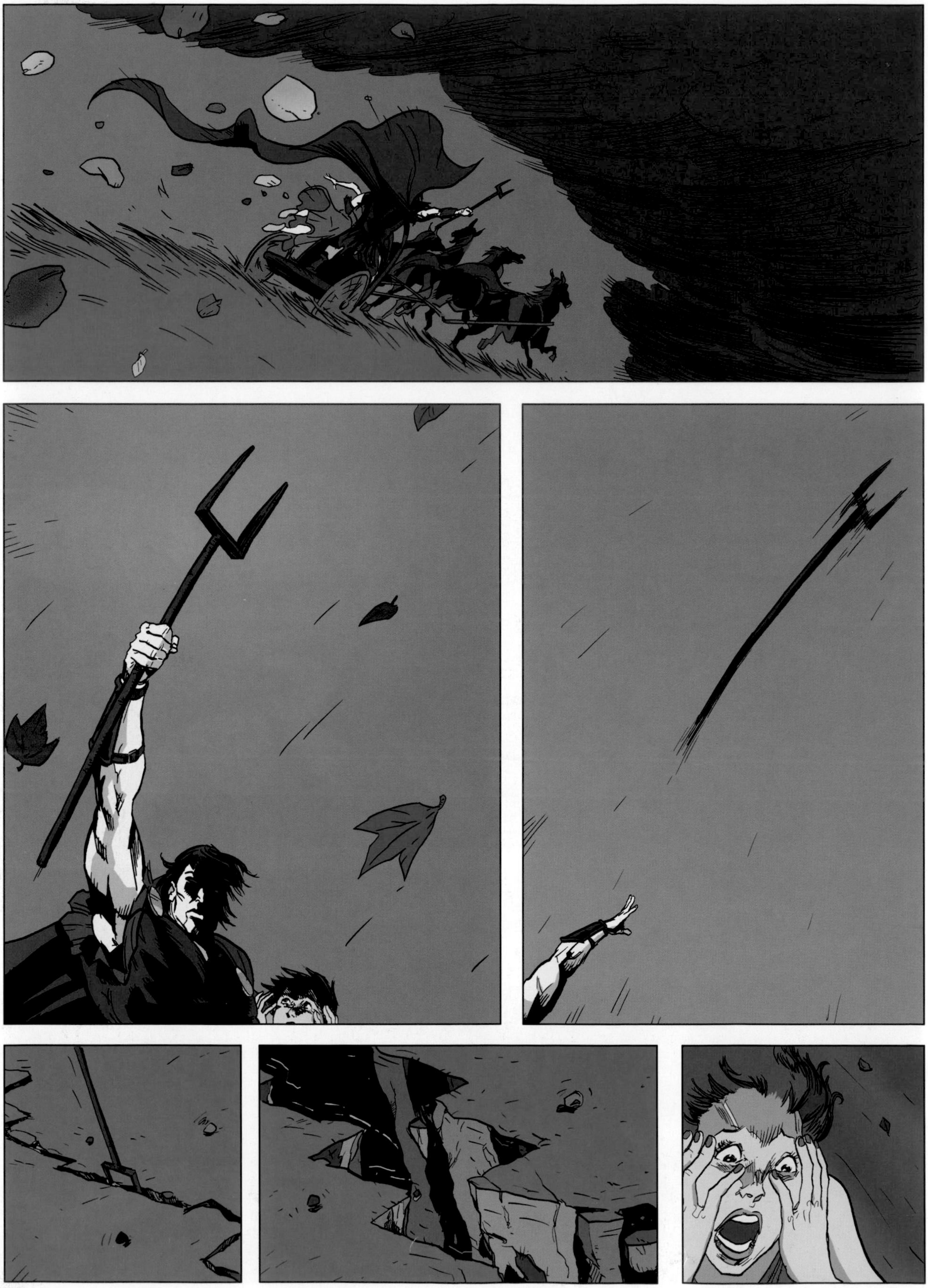

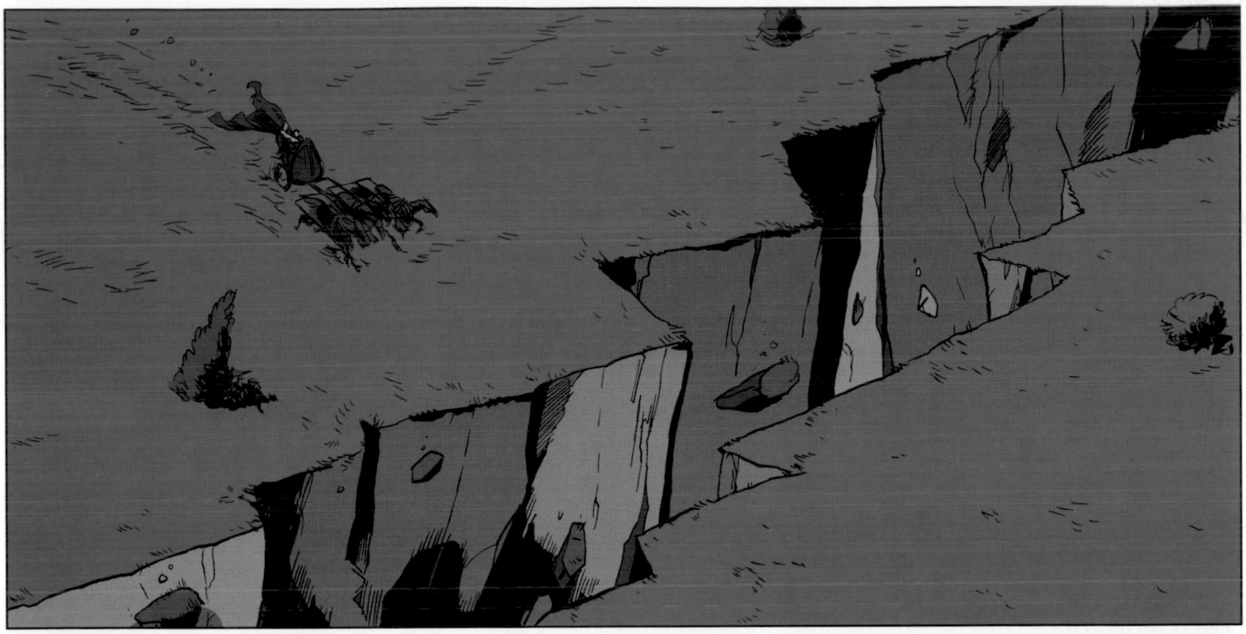

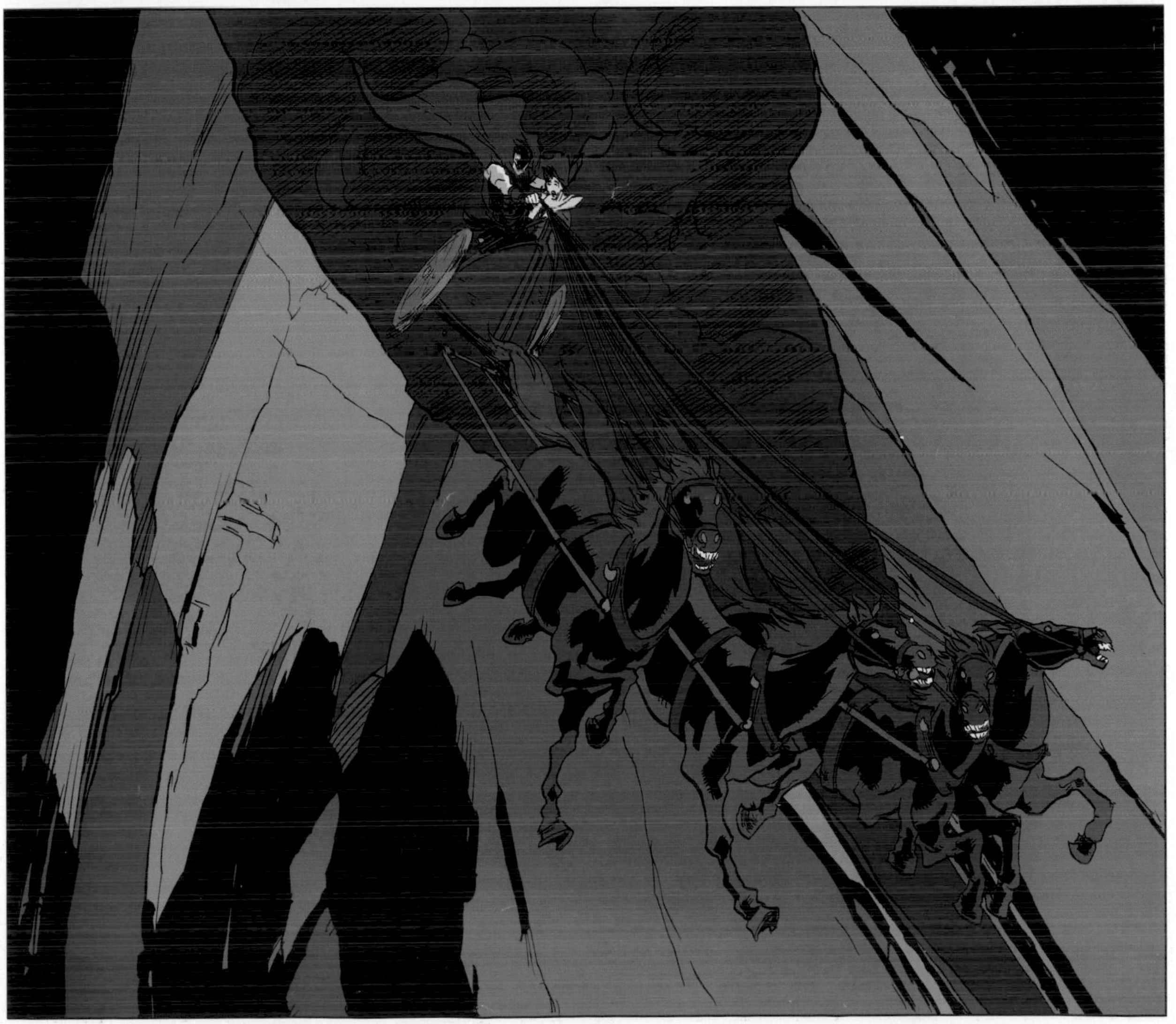

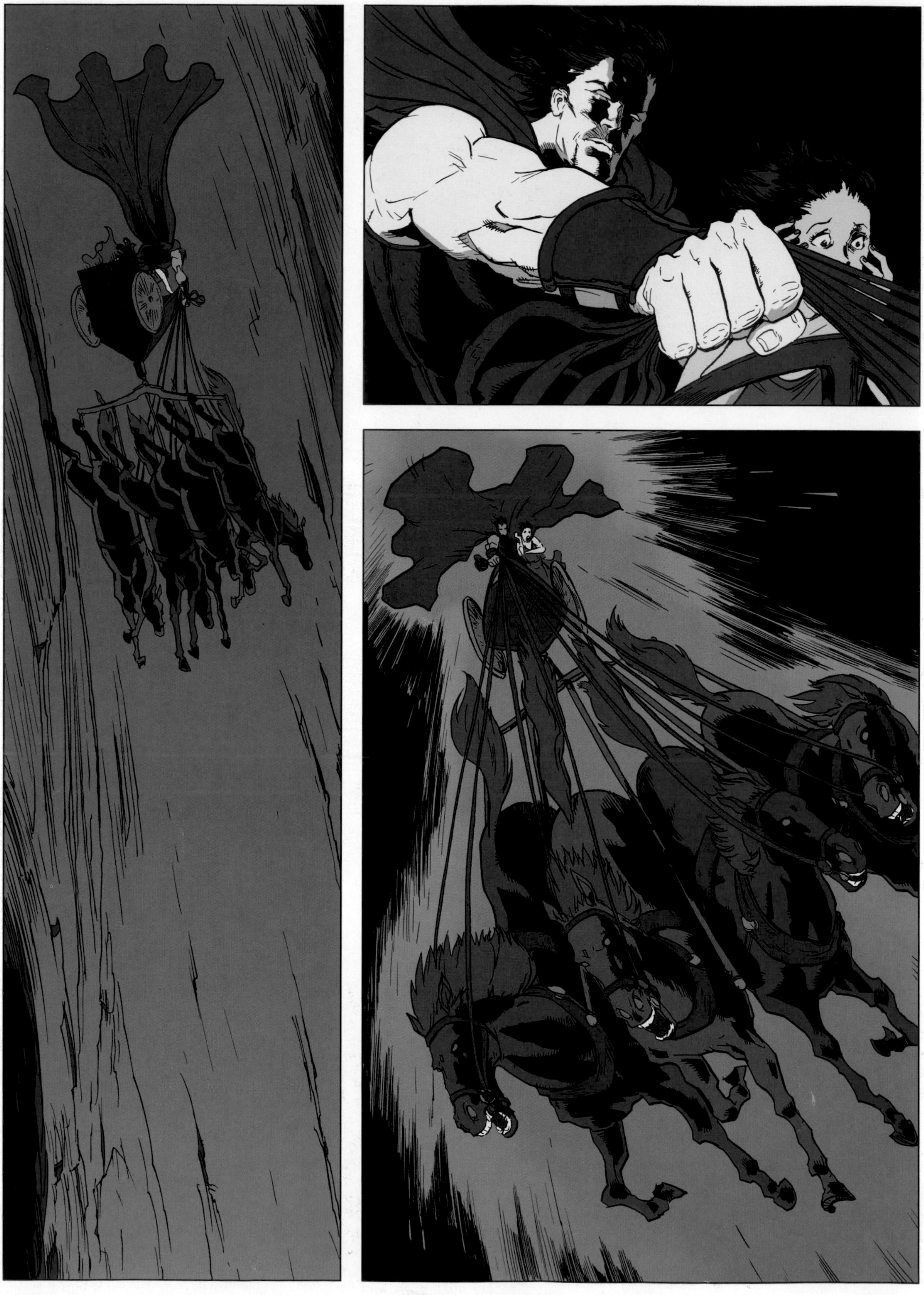

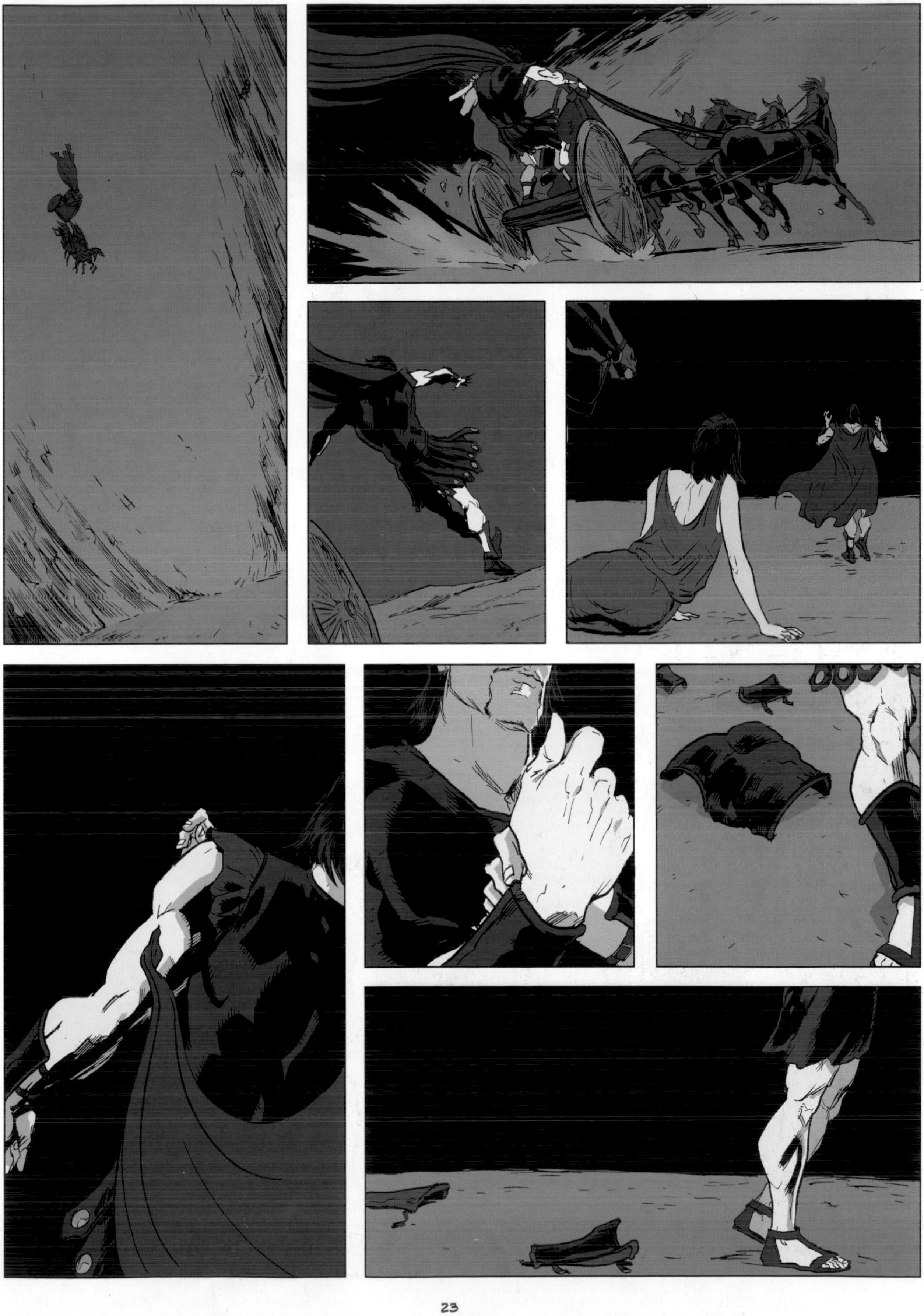

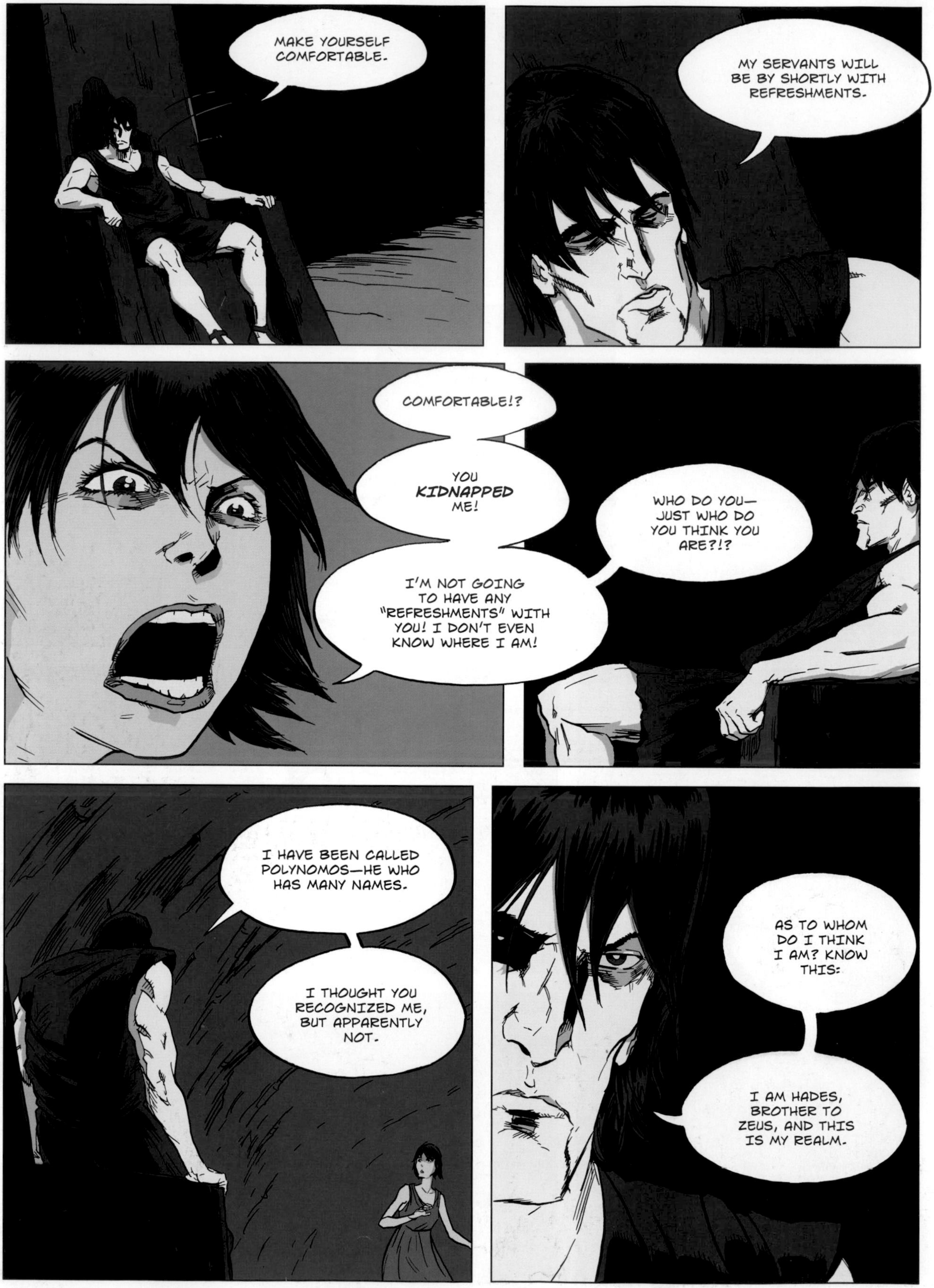
MAKE YOURSELF COMFORTABLE.
MY SERVANTS WILL BE BY SHORTLY WITH REFRESHMENTS.
COMFORTABLE!?
YOU **KIDNAPPED** ME!
I'M NOT GOING TO HAVE ANY "REFRESHMENTS" WITH YOU! I DON'T EVEN KNOW WHERE I AM!
WHO DO YOU— JUST WHO DO YOU THINK YOU ARE?!?
I HAVE BEEN CALLED POLYNOMOS—HE WHO HAS MANY NAMES.
I THOUGHT YOU RECOGNIZED ME, BUT APPARENTLY NOT.
AS TO WHOM DO I THINK I AM? KNOW THIS:
I AM HADES, BROTHER TO ZEUS, AND THIS IS MY REALM.

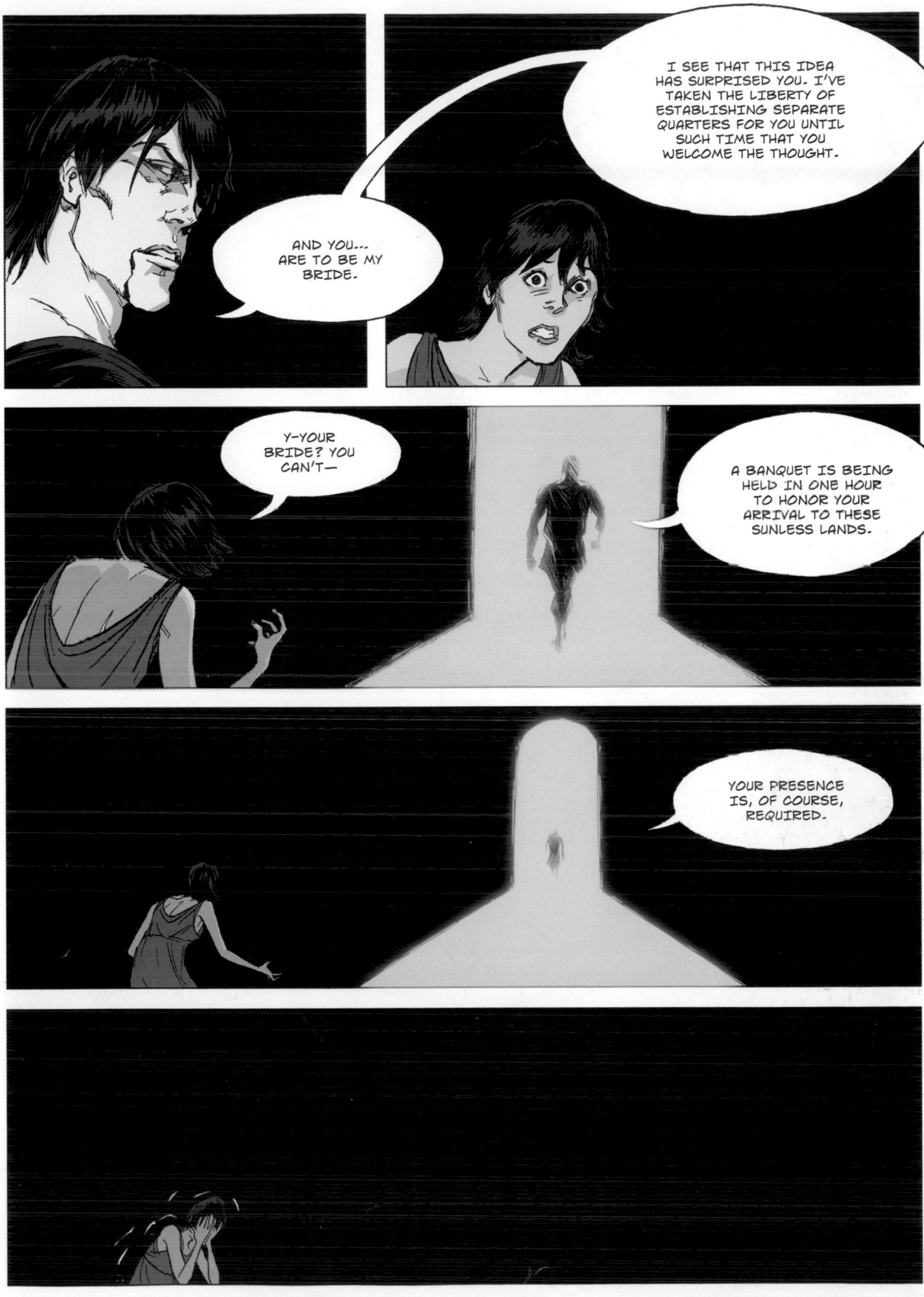
AND YOU... ARE TO BE MY BRIDE.
I SEE THAT THIS IDEA HAS SURPRISED YOU. I'VE TAKEN THE LIBERTY OF ESTABLISHING SEPARATE QUARTERS FOR YOU UNTIL SUCH TIME THAT YOU WELCOME THE THOUGHT.
Y-YOUR BRIDE? YOU CAN'T—
A BANQUET IS BEING HELD IN ONE HOUR TO HONOR YOUR ARRIVAL TO THESE SUNLESS LANDS.
YOUR PRESENCE IS, OF COURSE, REQUIRED.

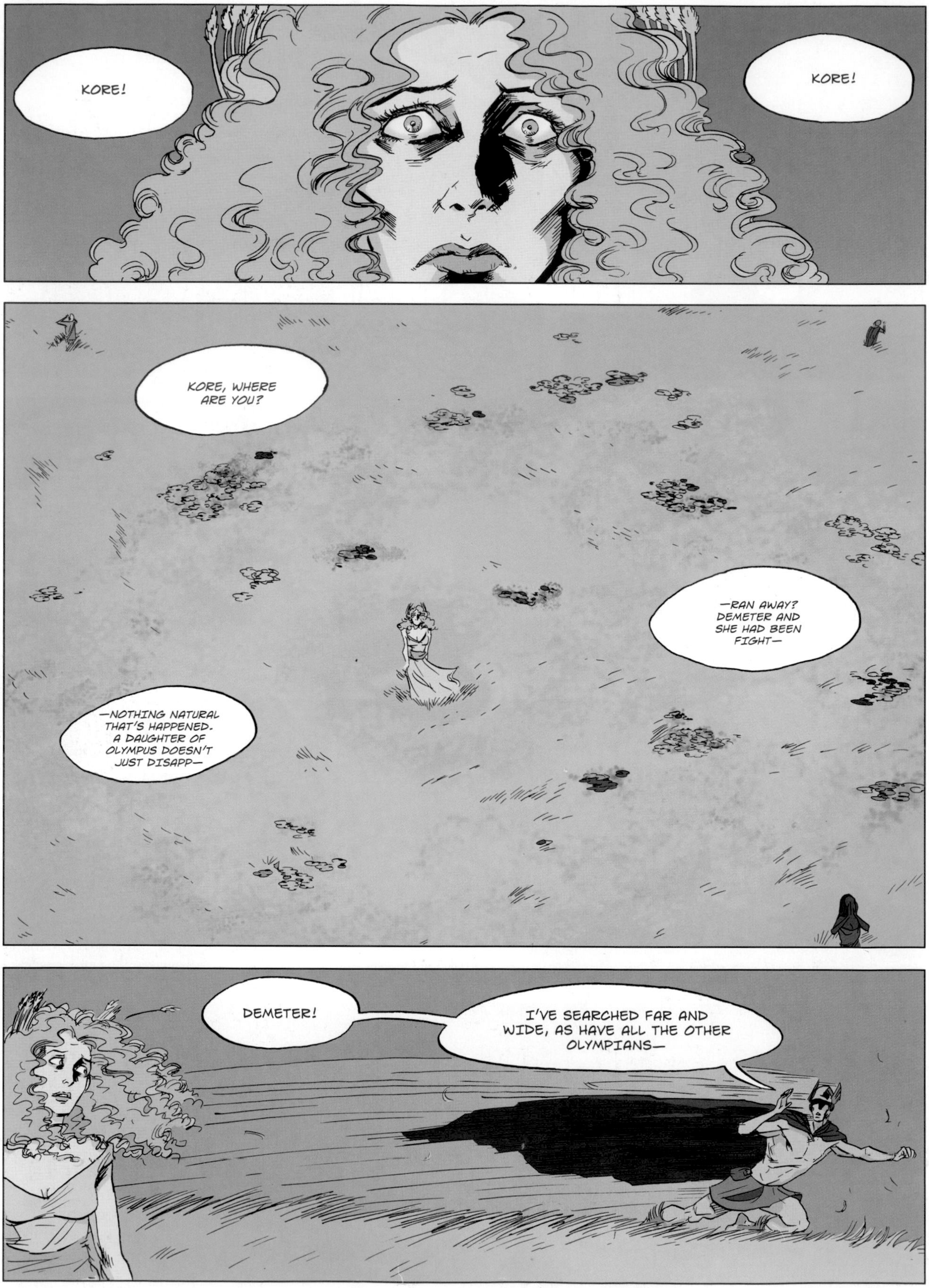
KORE!
KORE!
KORE, WHERE ARE YOU?
—RAN AWAY? DEMETER AND SHE HAD BEEN FIGHT—
—NOTHING NATURAL THAT'S HAPPENED. A DAUGHTER OF OLYMPUS DOESN'T JUST DISAPP—
DEMETER!
I'VE SEARCHED FAR AND WIDE, AS HAVE ALL THE OTHER OLYMPIANS—

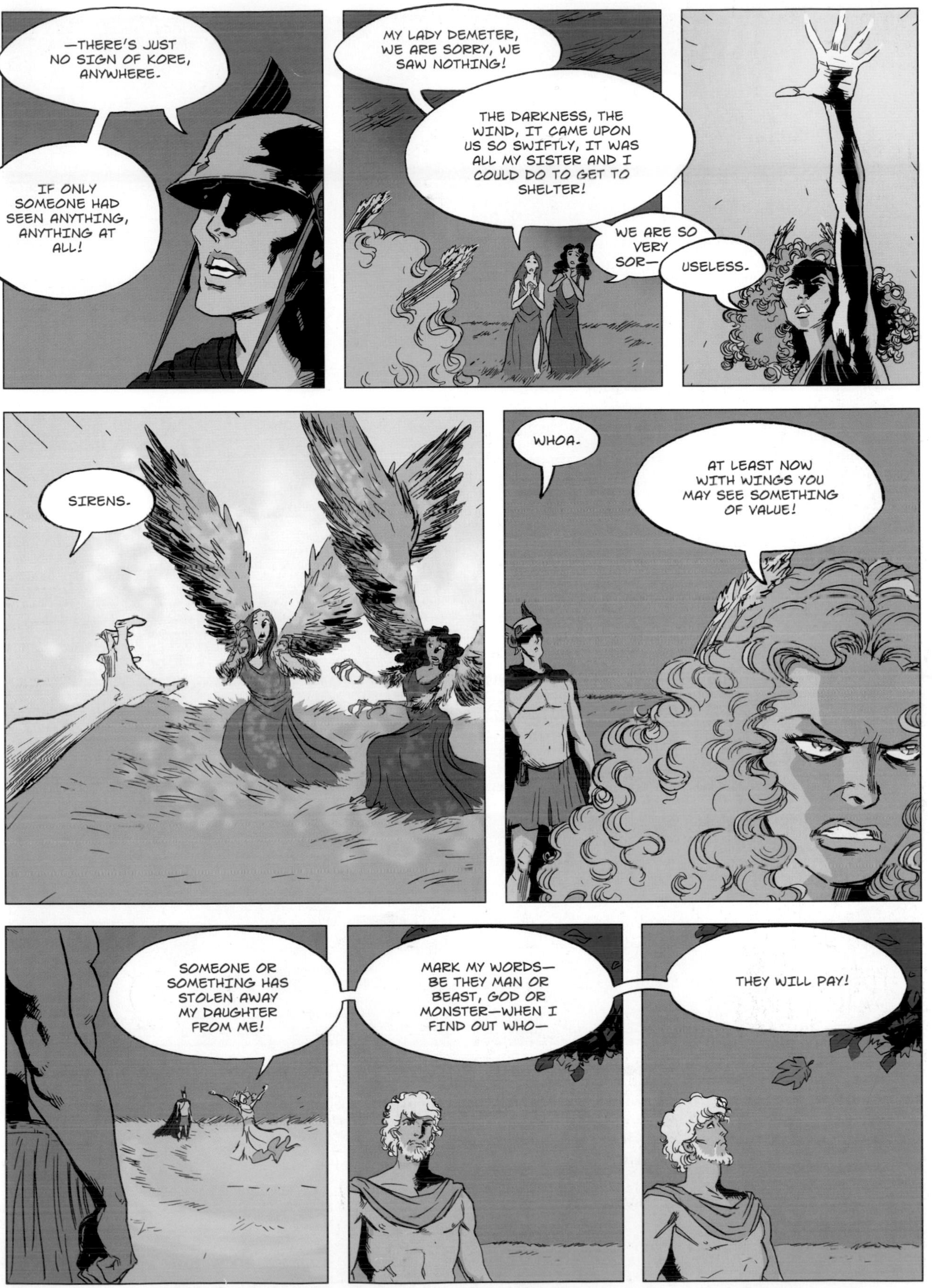
—THERE'S JUST NO SIGN OF KORE, ANYWHERE.
IF ONLY SOMEONE HAD SEEN ANYTHING, ANYTHING AT ALL!
MY LADY DEMETER, WE ARE SORRY, WE SAW NOTHING!
THE DARKNESS, THE WIND, IT CAME UPON US SO SWIFTLY, IT WAS ALL MY SISTER AND I COULD DO TO GET TO SHELTER!
WE ARE SO VERY SOR—
USELESS.
SIRENS.
WHOA.
AT LEAST NOW WITH WINGS YOU MAY SEE SOMETHING OF VALUE!
SOMEONE OR SOMETHING HAS STOLEN AWAY MY DAUGHTER FROM ME!
MARK MY WORDS—BE THEY MAN OR BEAST, GOD OR MONSTER—WHEN I FIND OUT WHO—
THEY WILL PAY!

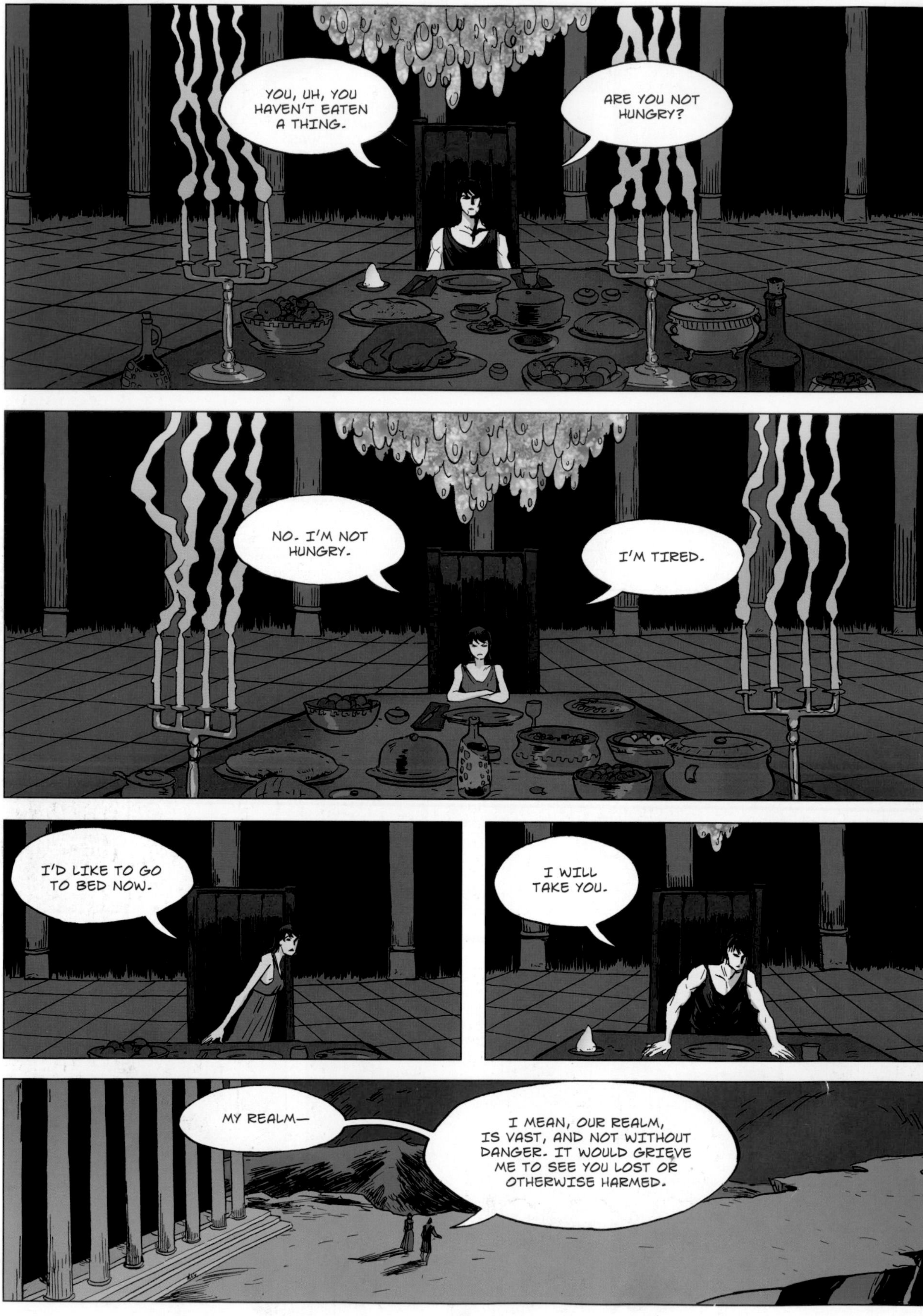
YOU, UH, YOU HAVEN'T EATEN A THING.
ARE YOU NOT HUNGRY?
NO. I'M NOT HUNGRY.
I'M TIRED.
I'D LIKE TO GO TO BED NOW.
I WILL TAKE YOU.
MY REALM—
I MEAN, OUR REALM, IS VAST, AND NOT WITHOUT DANGER. IT WOULD GRIEVE ME TO SEE YOU LOST OR OTHERWISE HARMED.

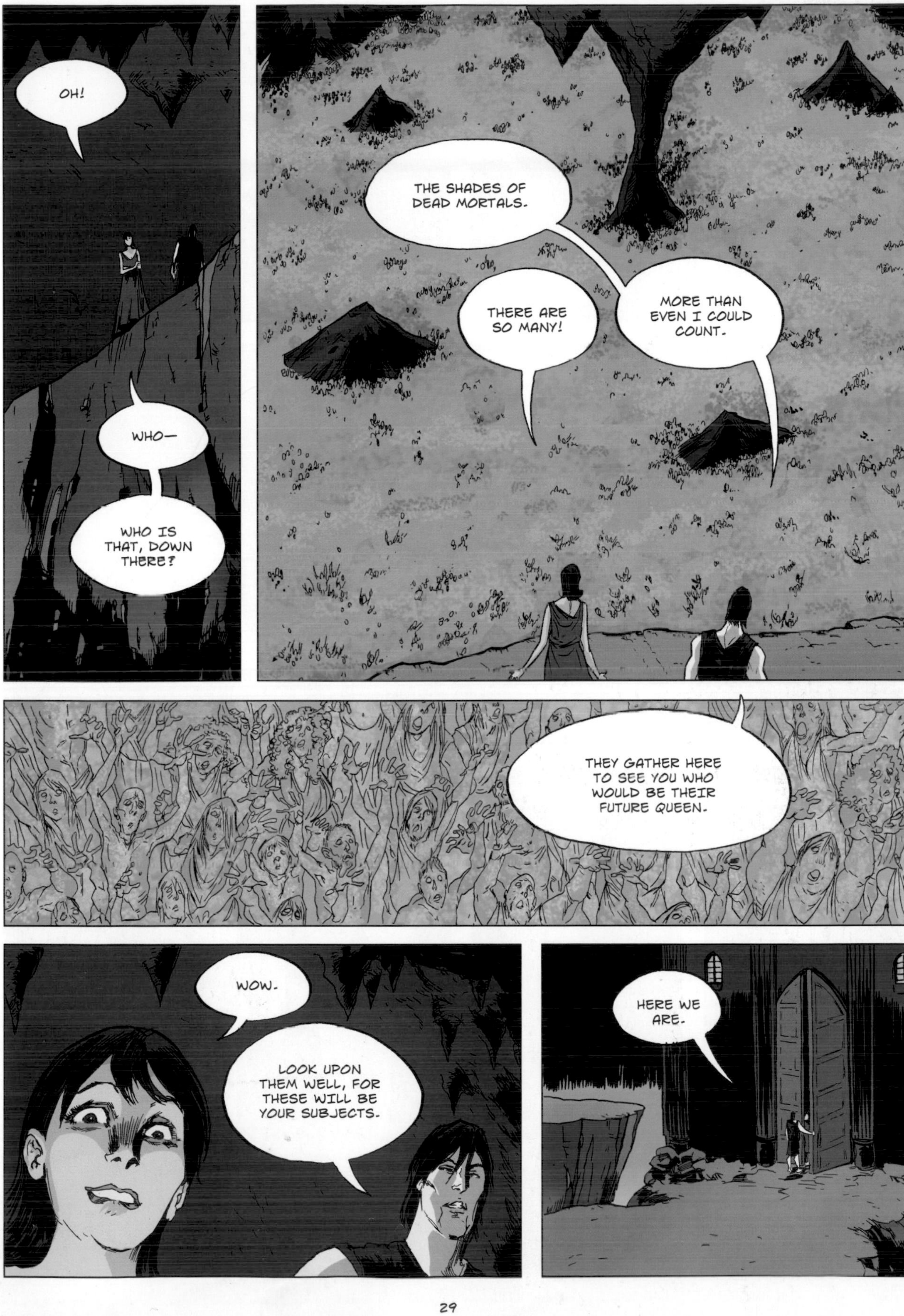
OH!
WHO—
WHO IS THAT, DOWN THERE?
THE SHADES OF DEAD MORTALS.
THERE ARE SO MANY!
MORE THAN EVEN I COULD COUNT.
THEY GATHER HERE TO SEE YOU WHO WOULD BE THEIR FUTURE QUEEN.
WOW.
LOOK UPON THEM WELL, FOR THESE WILL BE YOUR SUBJECTS.
HERE WE ARE.

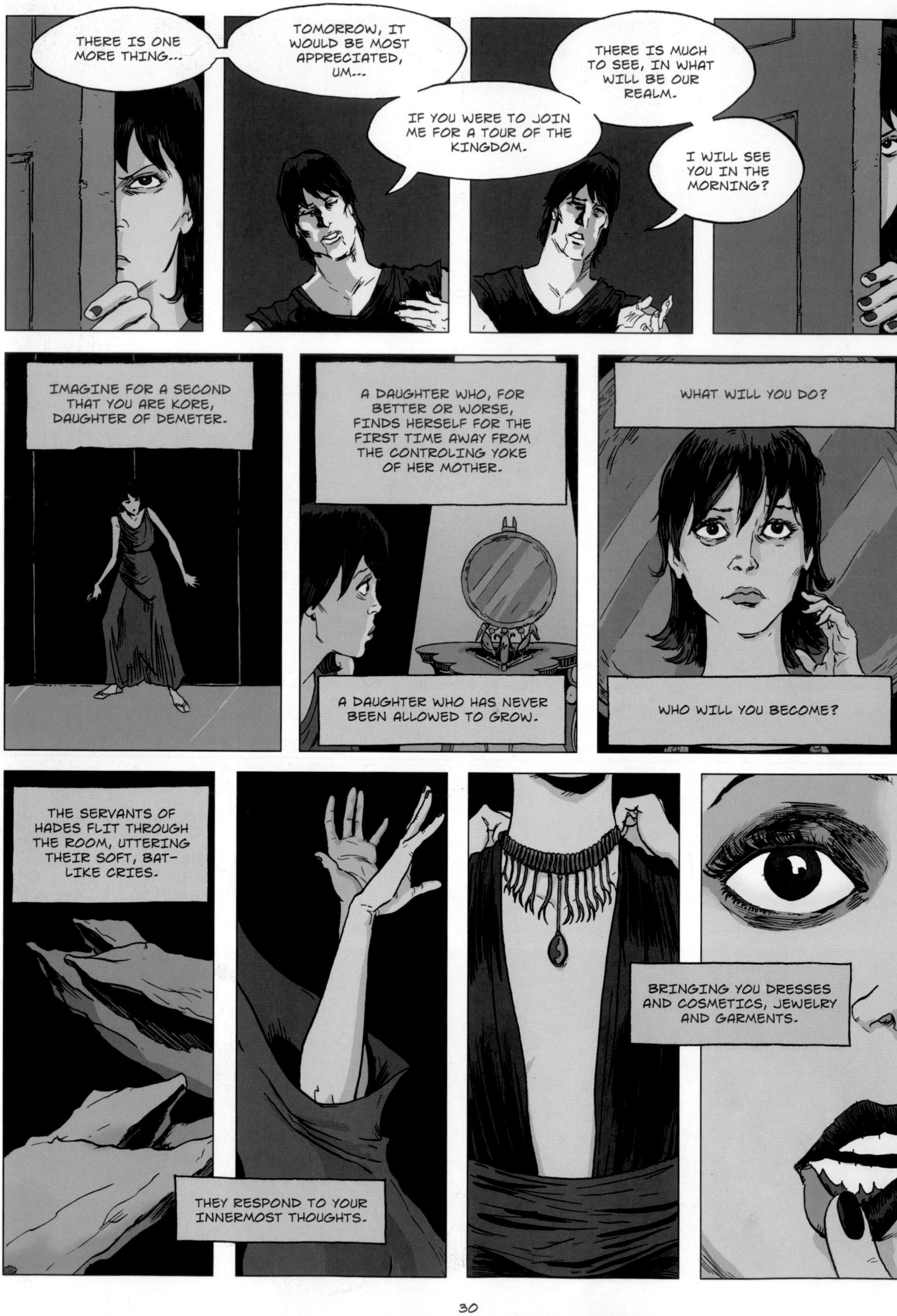

THERE IS ONE MORE THING...
TOMORROW, IT WOULD BE MOST APPRECIATED, UM...
IF YOU WERE TO JOIN ME FOR A TOUR OF THE KINGDOM.
THERE IS MUCH TO SEE, IN WHAT WILL BE OUR REALM.
I WILL SEE YOU IN THE MORNING?
IMAGINE FOR A SECOND THAT YOU ARE KORE, DAUGHTER OF DEMETER.
A DAUGHTER WHO, FOR BETTER OR WORSE, FINDS HERSELF FOR THE FIRST TIME AWAY FROM THE CONTROLING YOKE OF HER MOTHER.
A DAUGHTER WHO HAS NEVER BEEN ALLOWED TO GROW.
WHAT WILL YOU DO?
WHO WILL YOU BECOME?
THE SERVANTS OF HADES FLIT THROUGH THE ROOM, UTTERING THEIR SOFT, BAT-LIKE CRIES.
THEY RESPOND TO YOUR INNERMOST THOUGHTS.
BRINGING YOU DRESSES AND COSMETICS, JEWELRY AND GARMENTS.

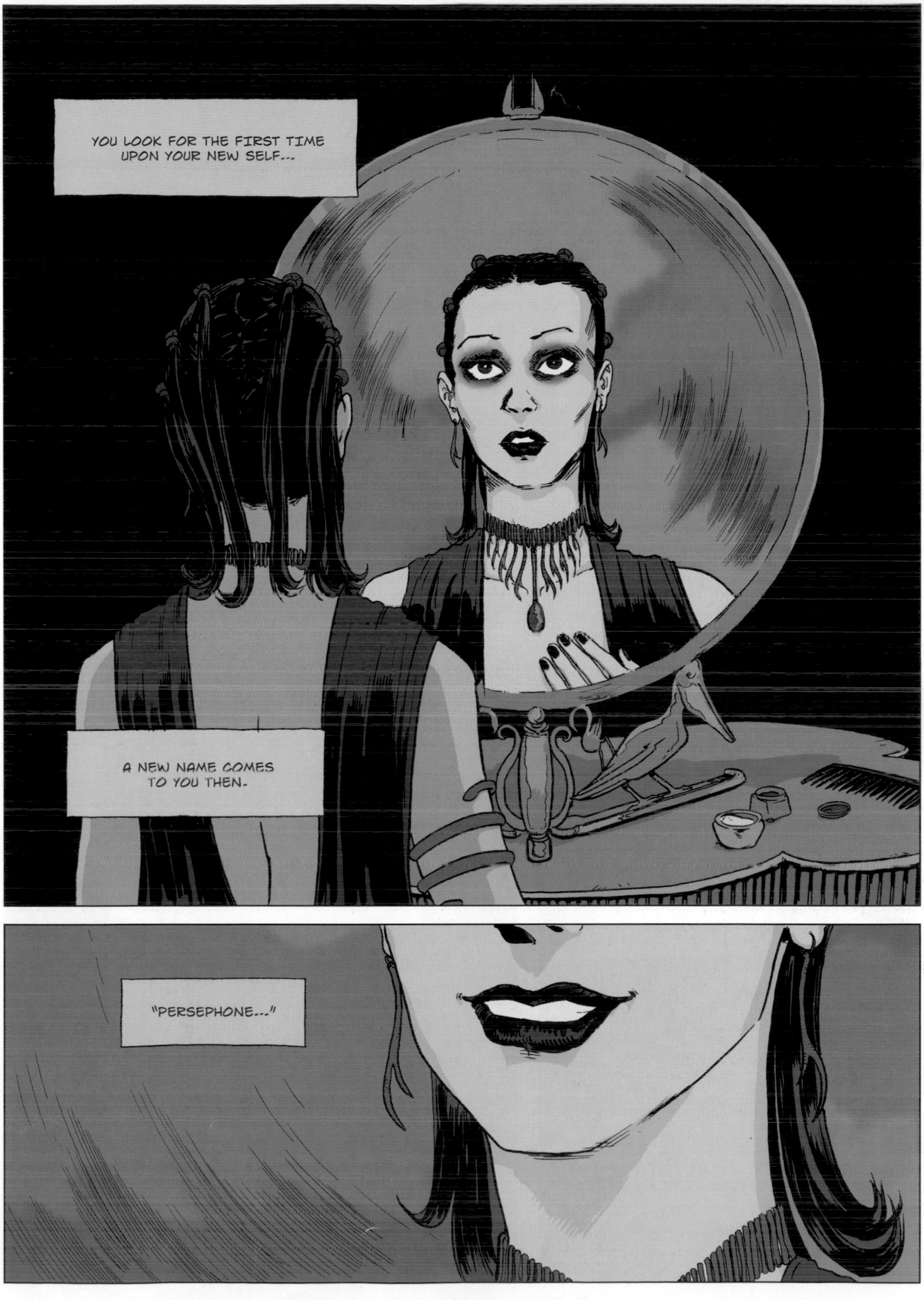
YOU LOOK FOR THE FIRST TIME UPON YOUR NEW SELF...
A NEW NAME COMES TO YOU THEN.
"PERSEPHONE..."

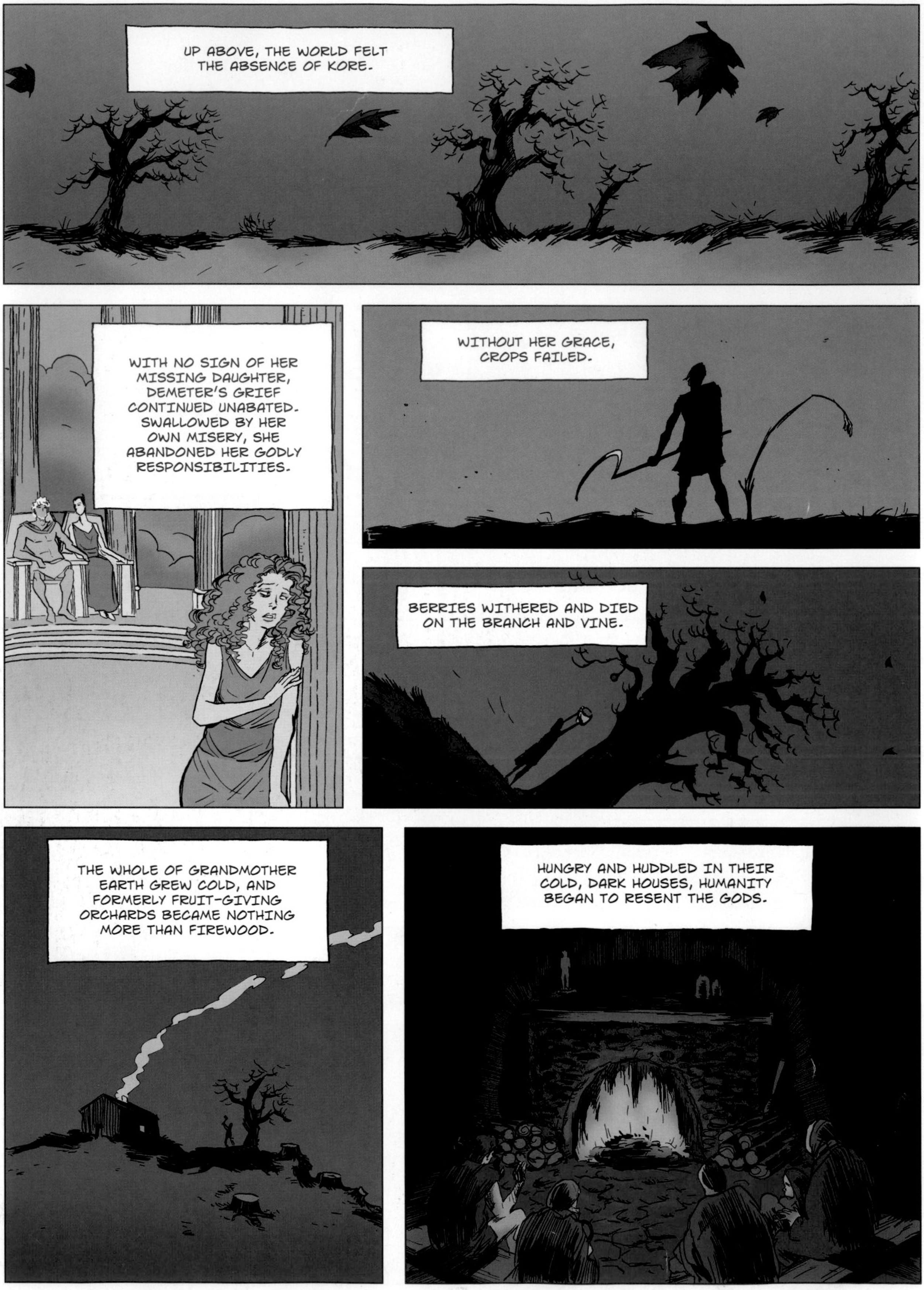
UP ABOVE, THE WORLD FELT THE ABSENCE OF KORE.
WITH NO SIGN OF HER MISSING DAUGHTER, DEMETER'S GRIEF CONTINUED UNABATED. SWALLOWED BY HER OWN MISERY, SHE ABANDONED HER GODLY RESPONSIBILITIES.
WITHOUT HER GRACE, CROPS FAILED.
BERRIES WITHERED AND DIED ON THE BRANCH AND VINE.
THE WHOLE OF GRANDMOTHER EARTH GREW COLD, AND FORMERLY FRUIT-GIVING ORCHARDS BECAME NOTHING MORE THAN FIREWOOD.
HUNGRY AND HUDDLED IN THEIR COLD, DARK HOUSES, HUMANITY BEGAN TO RESENT THE GODS.

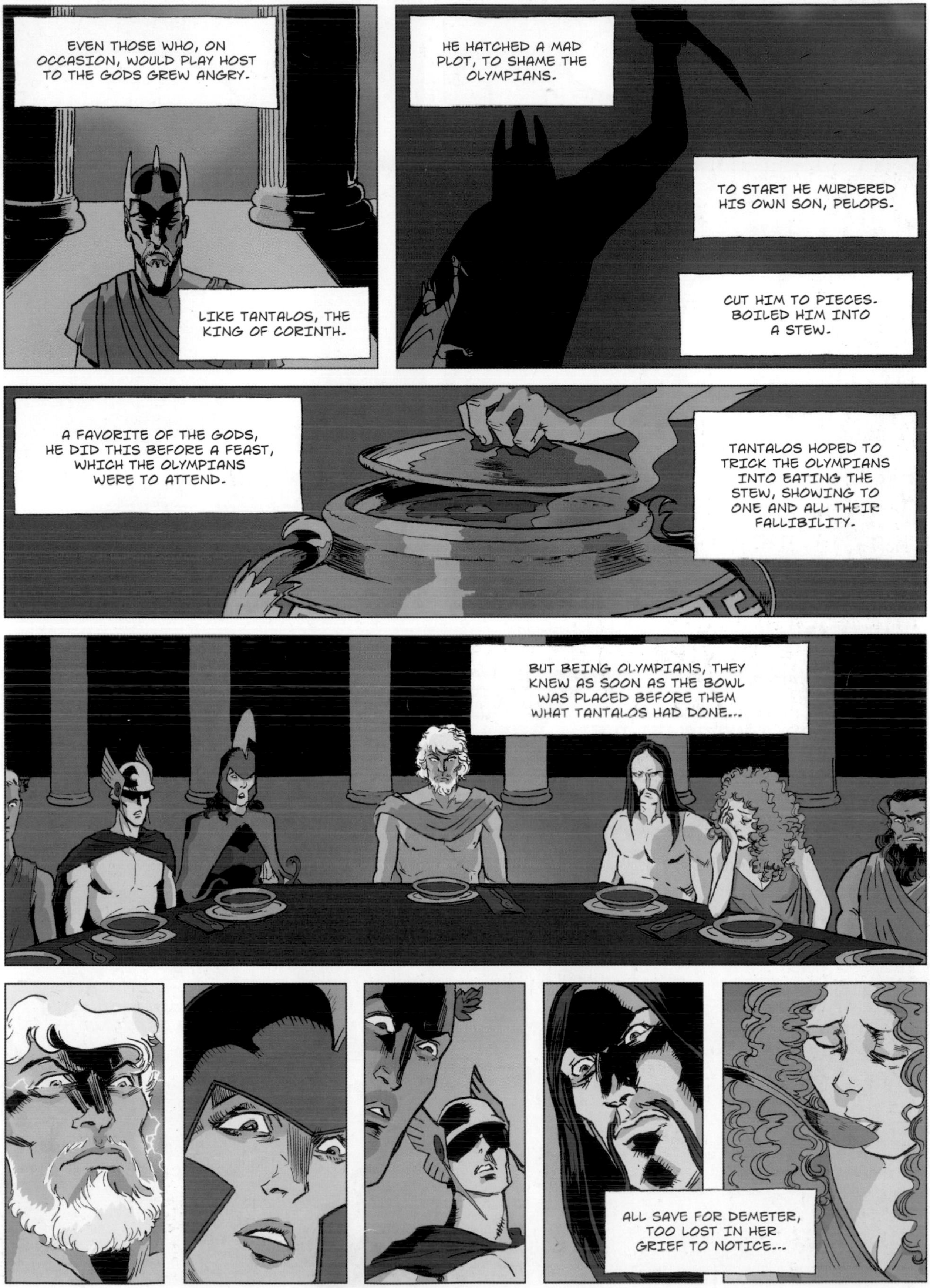
EVEN THOSE WHO, ON OCCASION, WOULD PLAY HOST TO THE GODS GREW ANGRY.
LIKE TANTALOS, THE KING OF CORINTH.
HE HATCHED A MAD PLOT, TO SHAME THE OLYMPIANS.
TO START HE MURDERED HIS OWN SON, PELOPS.
CUT HIM TO PIECES. BOILED HIM INTO A STEW.
A FAVORITE OF THE GODS, HE DID THIS BEFORE A FEAST, WHICH THE OLYMPIANS WERE TO ATTEND.
TANTALOS HOPED TO TRICK THE OLYMPIANS INTO EATING THE STEW, SHOWING TO ONE AND ALL THEIR FALLIBILITY.
BUT BEING OLYMPIANS, THEY KNEW AS SOON AS THE BOWL WAS PLACED BEFORE THEM WHAT TANTALOS HAD DONE...
ALL SAVE FOR DEMETER, TOO LOST IN HER GRIEF TO NOTICE...

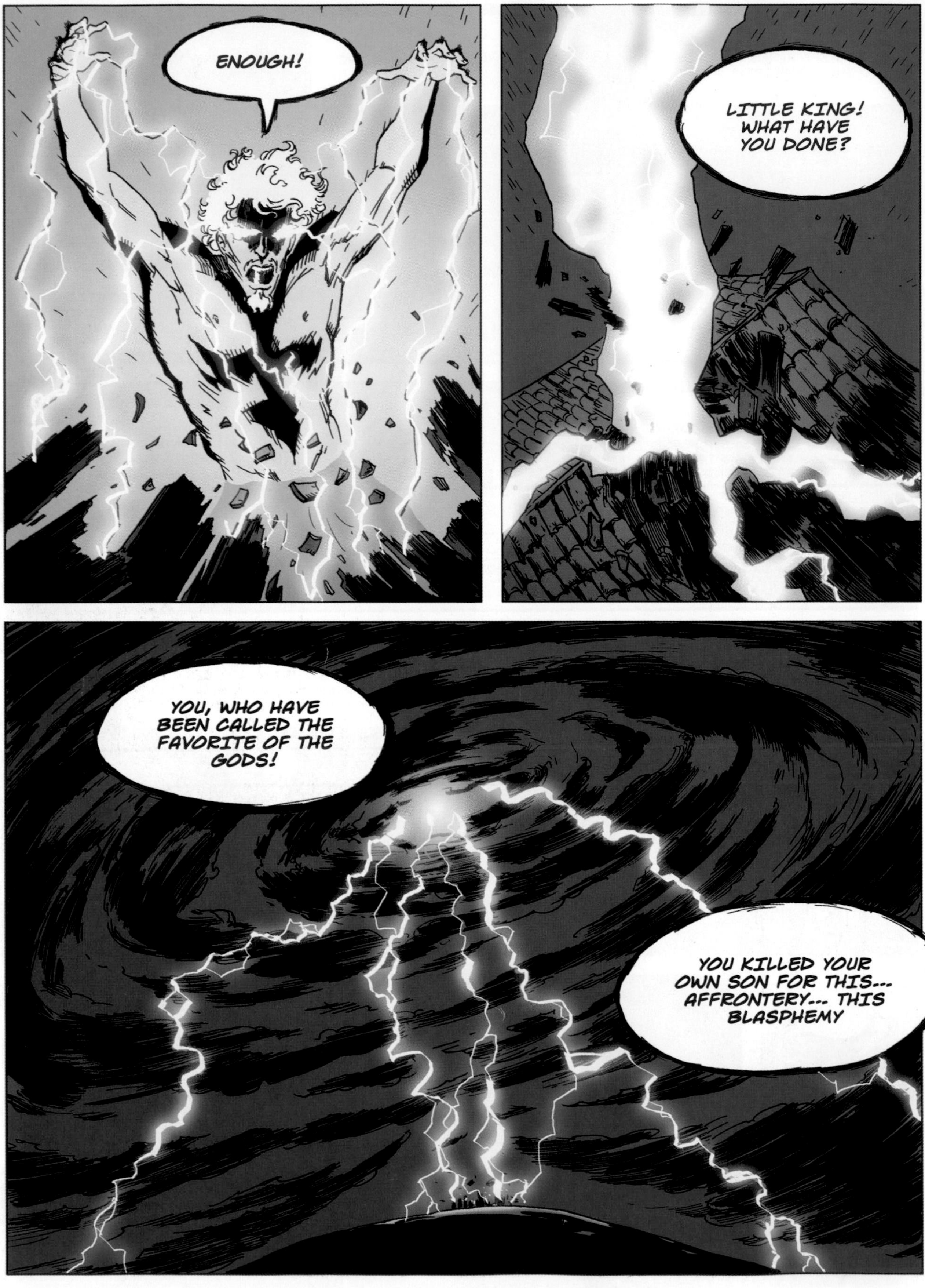
ENOUGH!
LITTLE KING! WHAT HAVE YOU DONE?
YOU, WHO HAVE BEEN CALLED THE FAVORITE OF THE GODS!
YOU KILLED YOUR OWN SON FOR THIS... AFFRONTERY... THIS BLASPHEMY

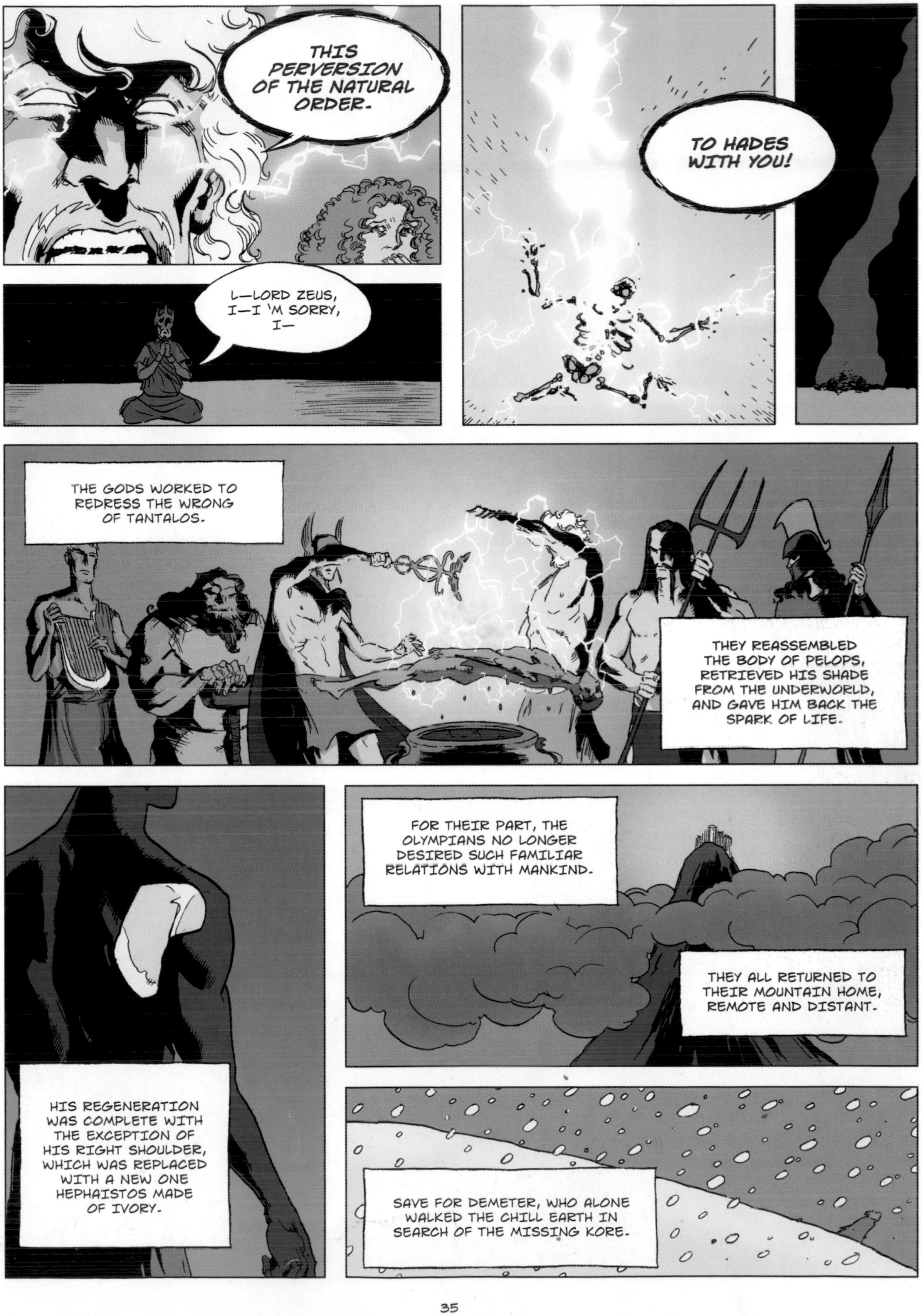

THIS PERVERSION OF THE NATURAL ORDER.
L—LORD ZEUS, I—I 'M SORRY, I—
TO HADES WITH YOU!
THE GODS WORKED TO REDRESS THE WRONG OF TANTALOS.
THEY REASSEMBLED THE BODY OF PELOPS, RETRIEVED HIS SHADE FROM THE UNDERWORLD, AND GAVE HIM BACK THE SPARK OF LIFE.
HIS REGENERATION WAS COMPLETE WITH THE EXCEPTION OF HIS RIGHT SHOULDER, WHICH WAS REPLACED WITH A NEW ONE HEPHAISTOS MADE OF IVORY.
FOR THEIR PART, THE OLYMPIANS NO LONGER DESIRED SUCH FAMILIAR RELATIONS WITH MANKIND.
THEY ALL RETURNED TO THEIR MOUNTAIN HOME, REMOTE AND DISTANT.
SAVE FOR DEMETER, WHO ALONE WALKED THE CHILL EARTH IN SEARCH OF THE MISSING KORE.

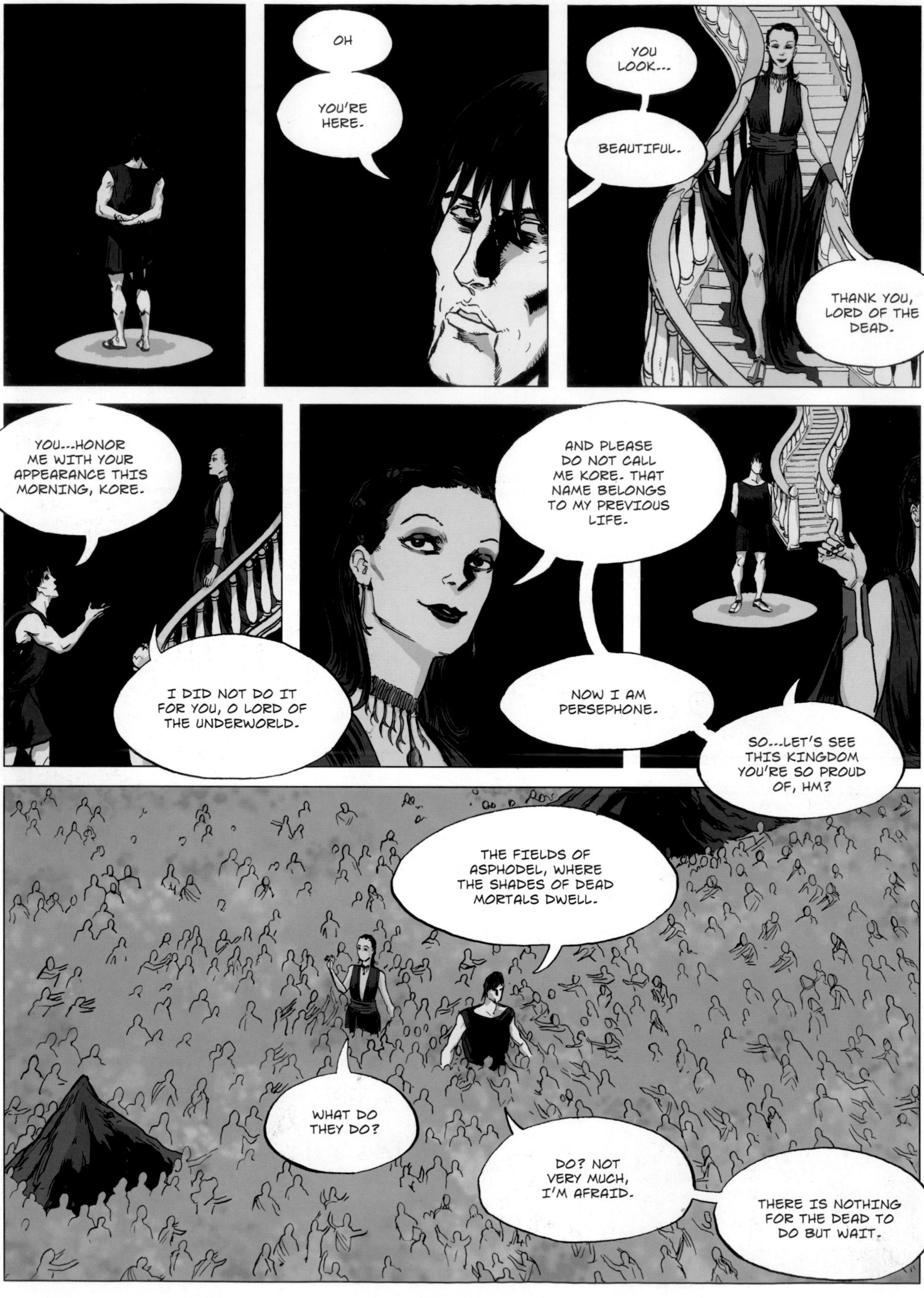
OH
YOU'RE HERE.
YOU LOOK...
BEAUTIFUL.
THANK YOU, LORD OF THE DEAD.
YOU...HONOR ME WITH YOUR APPEARANCE THIS MORNING, KORE.
I DID NOT DO IT FOR YOU, O LORD OF THE UNDERWORLD.
AND PLEASE DO NOT CALL ME KORE. THAT NAME BELONGS TO MY PREVIOUS LIFE.
NOW I AM PERSEPHONE.
SO...LET'S SEE THIS KINGDOM YOU'RE SO PROUD OF, HM?
THE FIELDS OF ASPHODEL, WHERE THE SHADES OF DEAD MORTALS DWELL.
WHAT DO THEY DO?
DO? NOT VERY MUCH, I'M AFRAID.
THERE IS NOTHING FOR THE DEAD TO DO BUT WAIT.

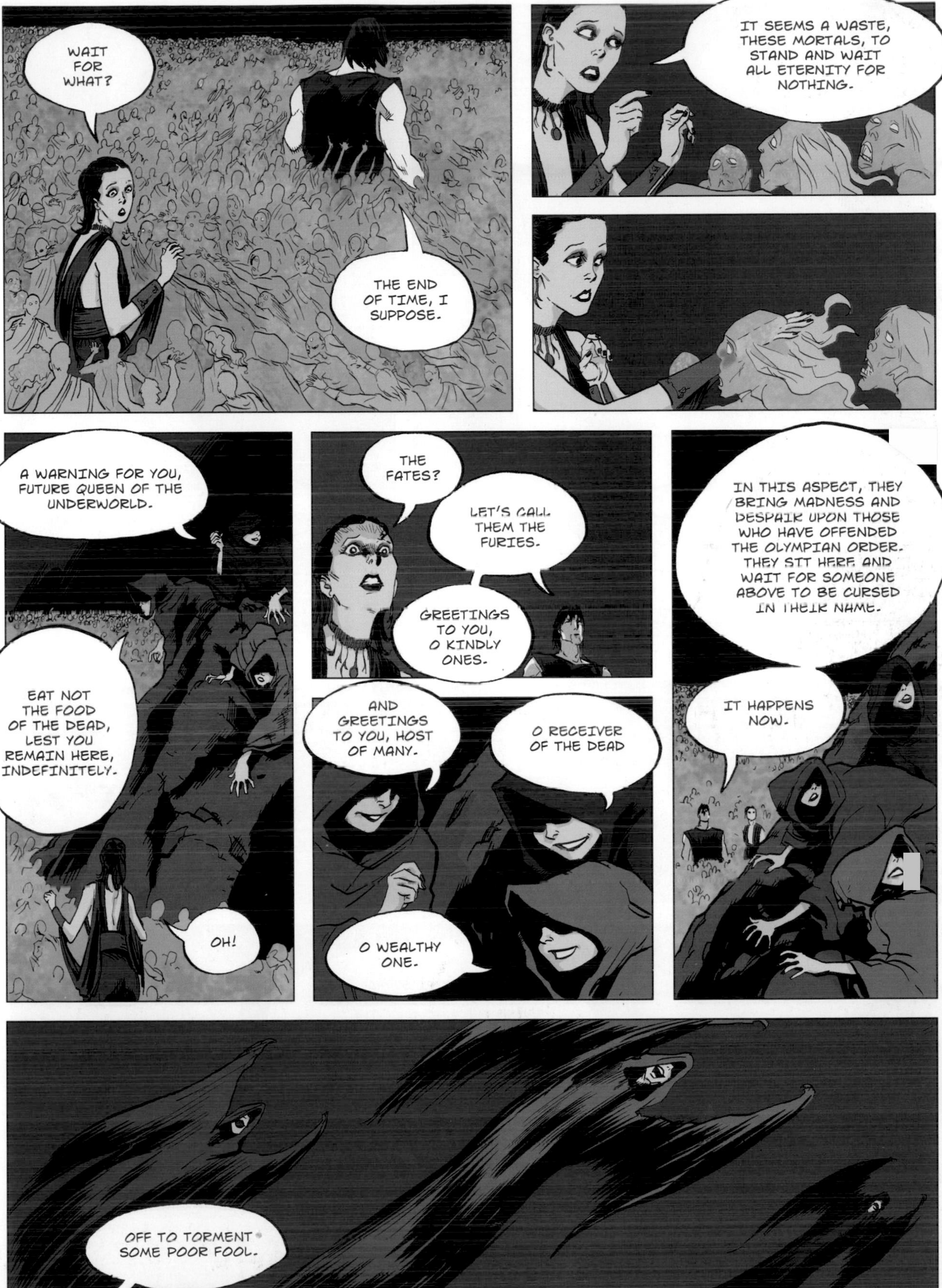
WAIT FOR WHAT?
THE END OF TIME, I SUPPOSE.
IT SEEMS A WASTE, THESE MORTALS, TO STAND AND WAIT ALL ETERNITY FOR NOTHING.
A WARNING FOR YOU, FUTURE QUEEN OF THE UNDERWORLD.
EAT NOT THE FOOD OF THE DEAD, LEST YOU REMAIN HERE, INDEFINITELY.
OH!
THE FATES?
LET'S CALL THEM THE FURIES.
GREETINGS TO YOU, O KINDLY ONES.
AND GREETINGS TO YOU, HOST OF MANY.
O RECEIVER OF THE DEAD
O WEALTHY ONE.
IN THIS ASPECT, THEY BRING MADNESS AND DESPAIR UPON THOSE WHO HAVE OFFENDED THE OLYMPIAN ORDER. THEY SIT HERE AND WAIT FOR SOMEONE ABOVE TO BE CURSED IN THEIR NAME.
IT HAPPENS NOW.
OFF TO TORMENT SOME POOR FOOL.

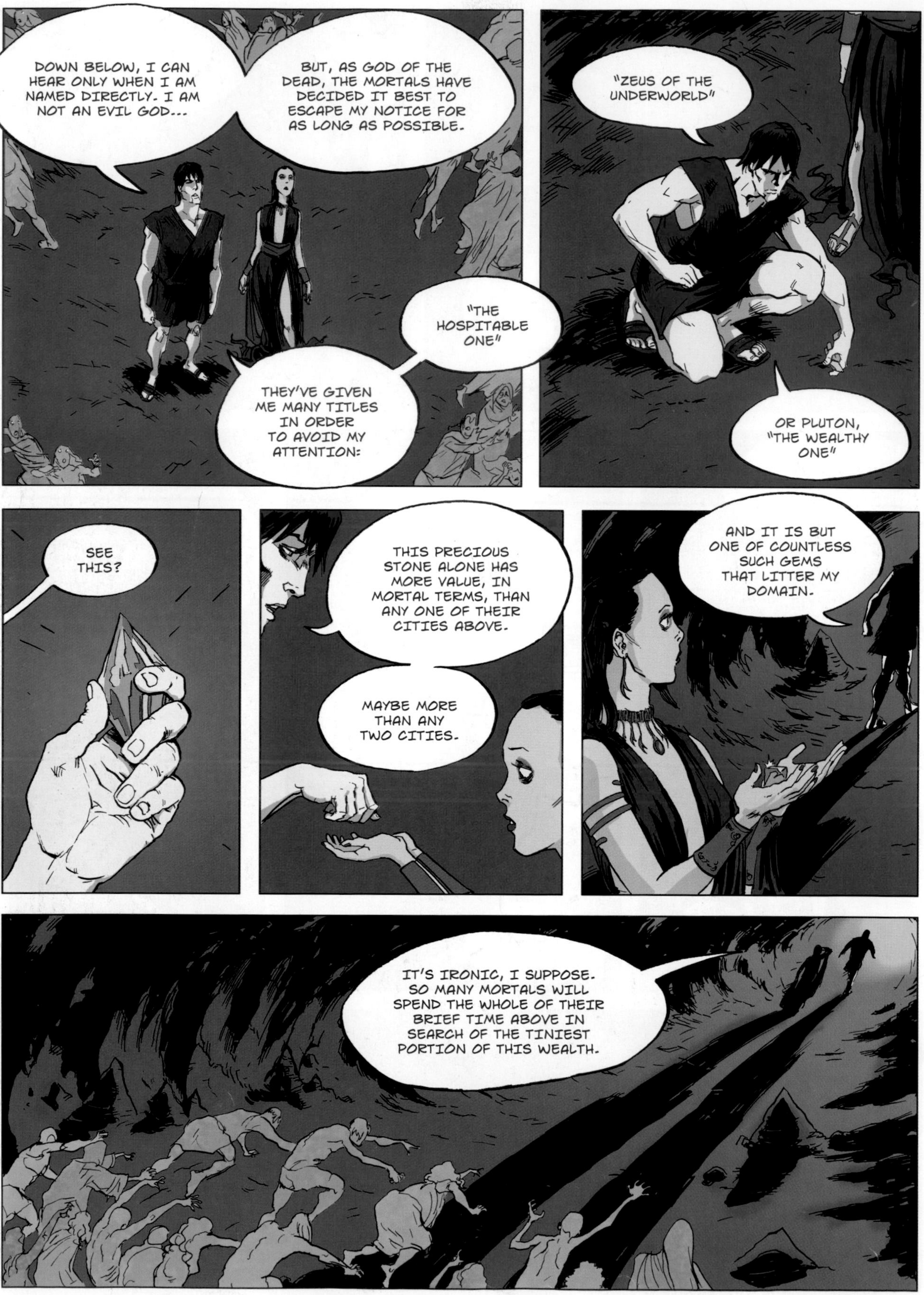
DOWN BELOW, I CAN HEAR ONLY WHEN I AM NAMED DIRECTLY. I AM NOT AN EVIL GOD...
BUT, AS GOD OF THE DEAD, THE MORTALS HAVE DECIDED IT BEST TO ESCAPE MY NOTICE FOR AS LONG AS POSSIBLE.
THEY'VE GIVEN ME MANY TITLES IN ORDER TO AVOID MY ATTENTION:
"THE HOSPITABLE ONE"
"ZEUS OF THE UNDERWORLD"
OR PLUTON, "THE WEALTHY ONE"
SEE THIS?
THIS PRECIOUS STONE ALONE HAS MORE VALUE, IN MORTAL TERMS, THAN ANY ONE OF THEIR CITIES ABOVE.
MAYBE MORE THAN ANY TWO CITIES.
AND IT IS BUT ONE OF COUNTLESS SUCH GEMS THAT LITTER MY DOMAIN.
IT'S IRONIC, I SUPPOSE. SO MANY MORTALS WILL SPEND THE WHOLE OF THEIR BRIEF TIME ABOVE IN SEARCH OF THE TINIEST PORTION OF THIS WEALTH.

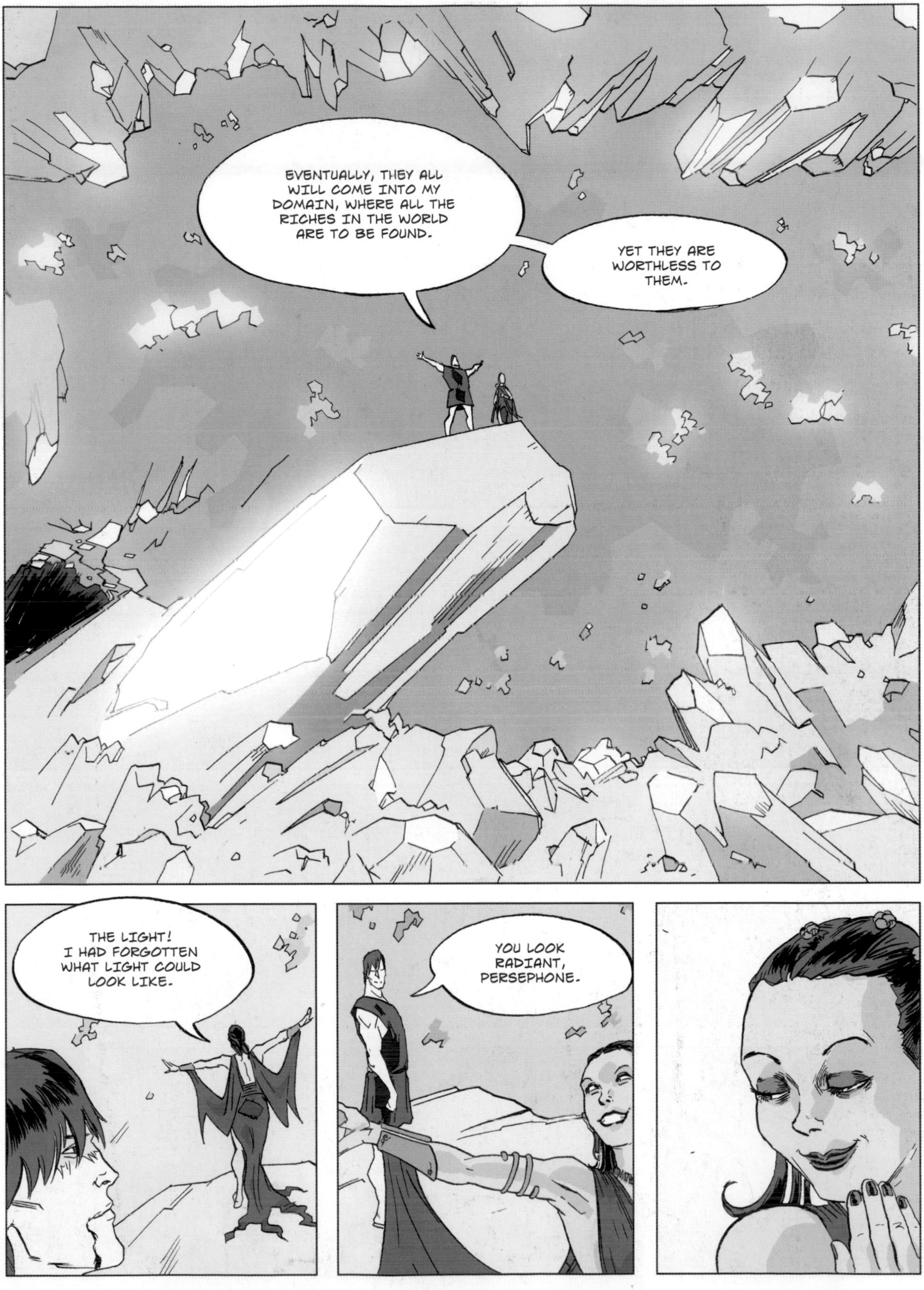
EVENTUALLY, THEY ALL WILL COME INTO MY DOMAIN, WHERE ALL THE RICHES IN THE WORLD ARE TO BE FOUND.
YET THEY ARE WORTHLESS TO THEM.
THE LIGHT! I HAD FORGOTTEN WHAT LIGHT COULD LOOK LIKE.
YOU LOOK RADIANT, PERSEPHONE.

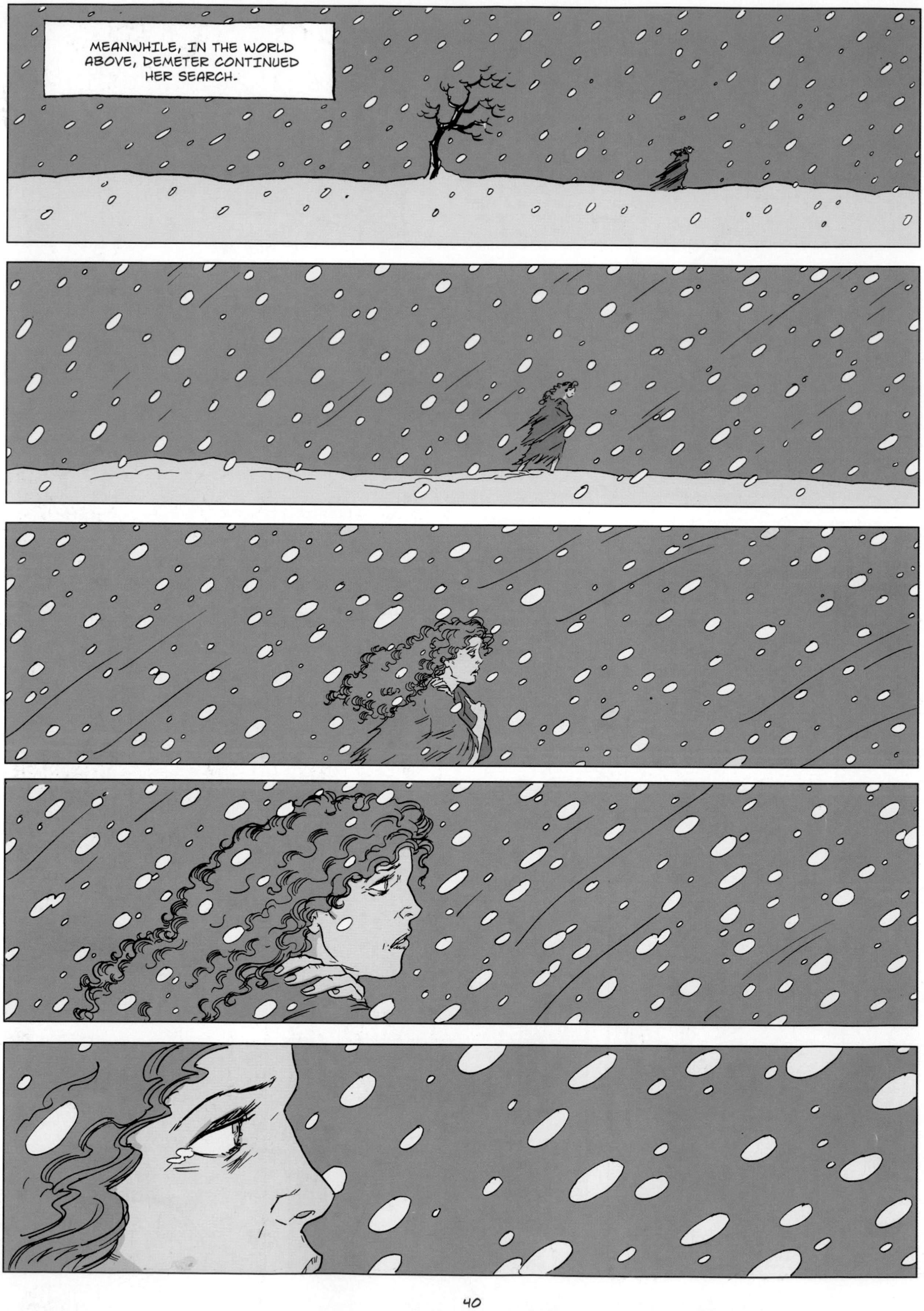
MEANWHILE, IN THE WORLD ABOVE, DEMETER CONTINUED HER SEARCH.

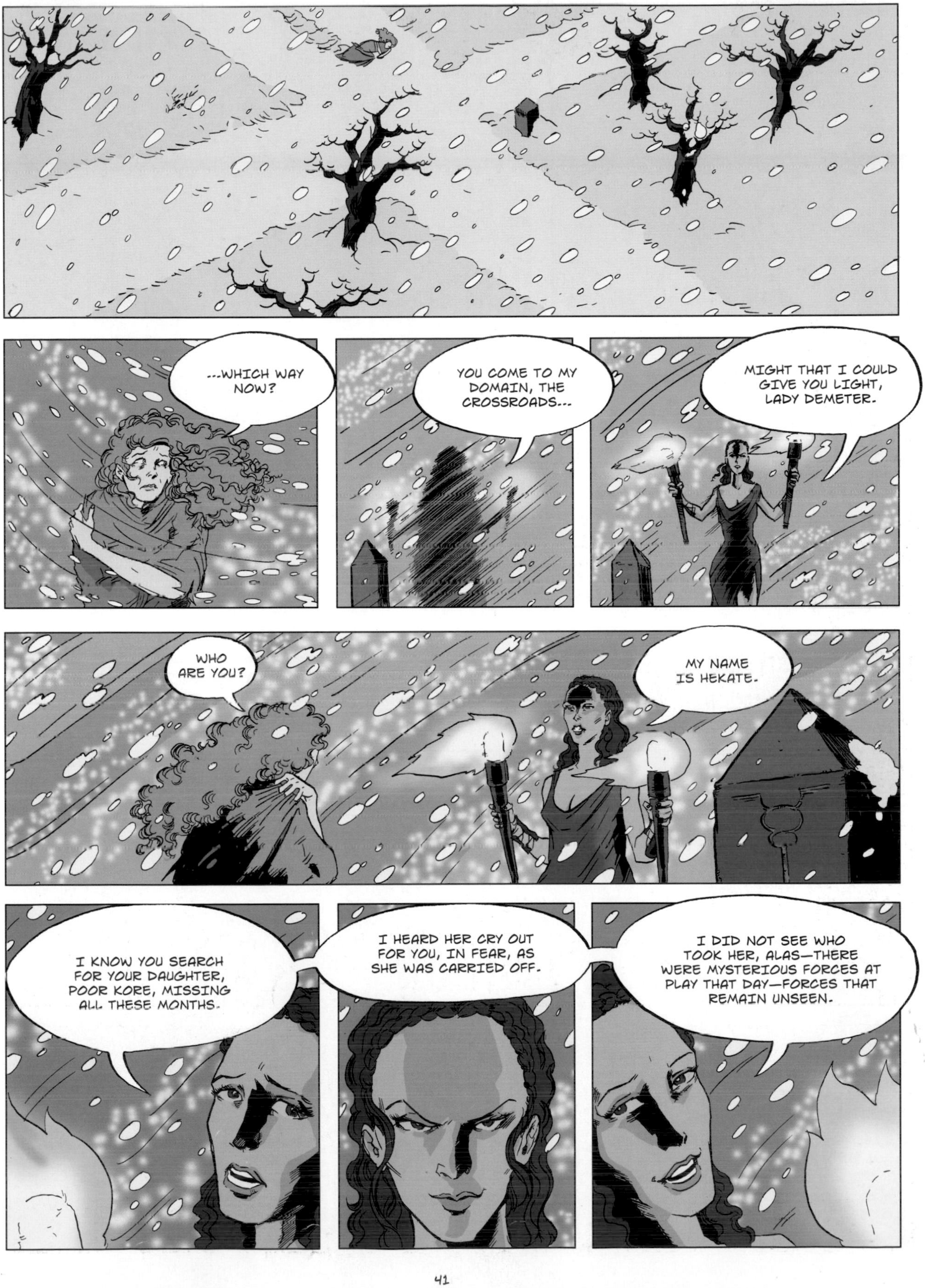

...WHICH WAY NOW?
YOU COME TO MY DOMAIN, THE CROSSROADS...
MIGHT THAT I COULD GIVE YOU LIGHT, LADY DEMETER.
WHO ARE YOU?
MY NAME IS HEKATE.
I KNOW YOU SEARCH FOR YOUR DAUGHTER, POOR KORE, MISSING ALL THESE MONTHS.
I HEARD HER CRY OUT FOR YOU, IN FEAR, AS SHE WAS CARRIED OFF.
I DID NOT SEE WHO TOOK HER, ALAS—THERE WERE MYSTERIOUS FORCES AT PLAY THAT DAY—FORCES THAT REMAIN UNSEEN.

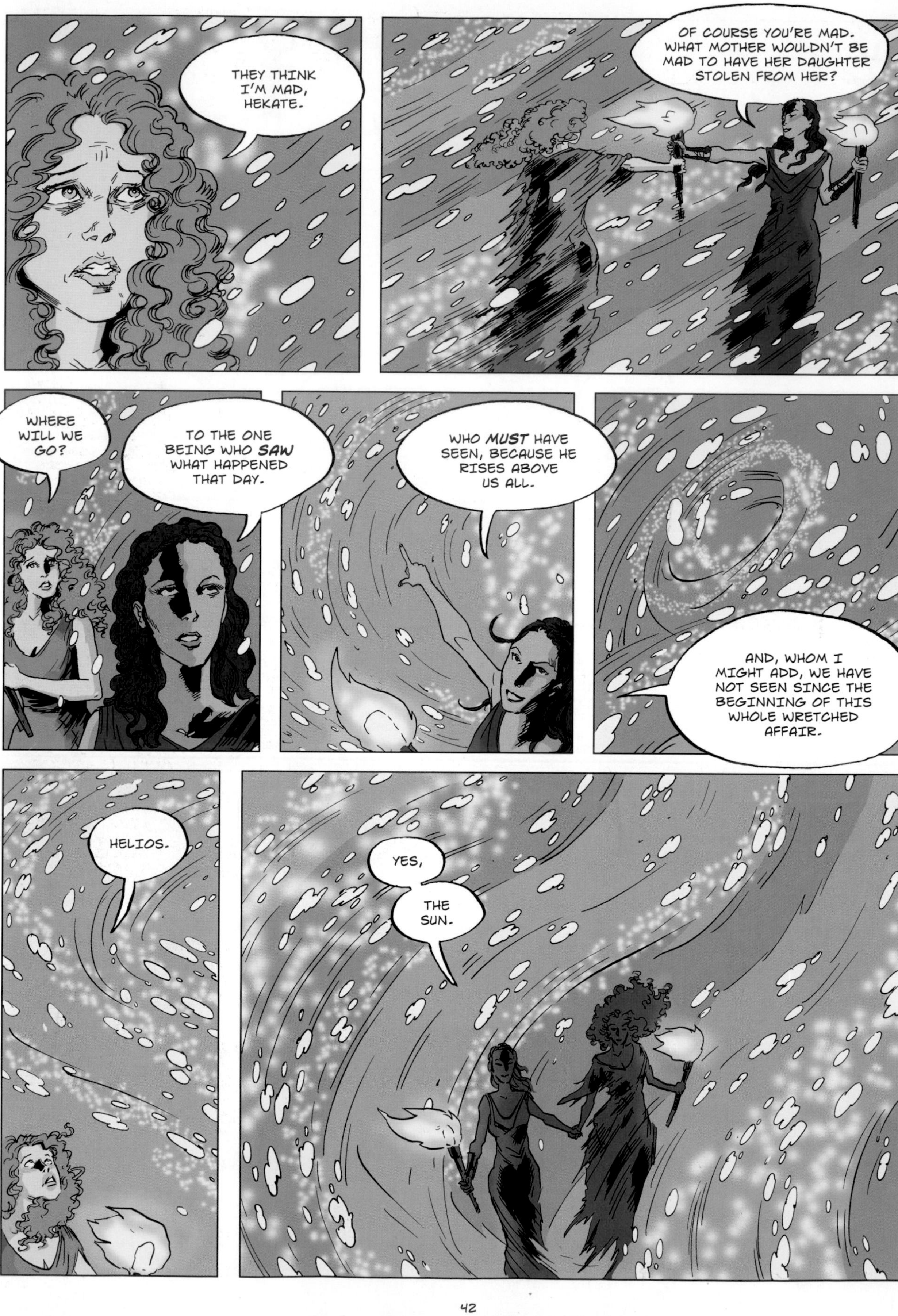

THEY THINK I'M MAD, HEKATE.
OF COURSE YOU'RE MAD. WHAT MOTHER WOULDN'T BE MAD TO HAVE HER DAUGHTER STOLEN FROM HER?
WHERE WILL WE GO?
TO THE ONE BEING WHO SAW WHAT HAPPENED THAT DAY.
WHO MUST HAVE SEEN, BECAUSE HE RISES ABOVE US ALL.
AND, WHOM I MIGHT ADD, WE HAVE NOT SEEN SINCE THE BEGINNING OF THIS WHOLE WRETCHED AFFAIR.
HELIOS.
YES,
THE SUN.

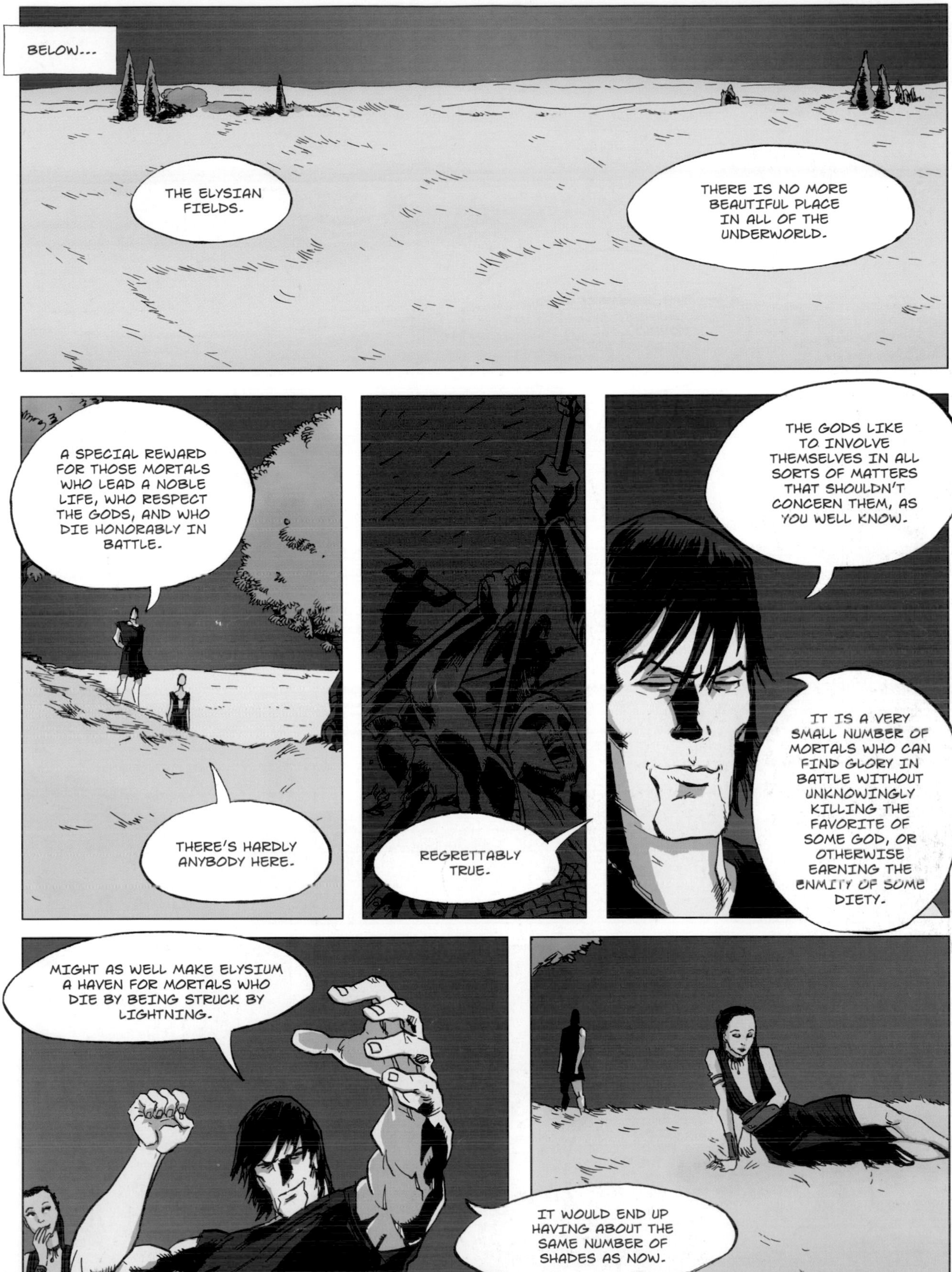
BELOW...
THE ELYSIAN FIELDS.
THERE IS NO MORE BEAUTIFUL PLACE IN ALL OF THE UNDERWORLD.
A SPECIAL REWARD FOR THOSE MORTALS WHO LEAD A NOBLE LIFE, WHO RESPECT THE GODS, AND WHO DIE HONORABLY IN BATTLE.
THERE'S HARDLY ANYBODY HERE.
REGRETTABLY TRUE.
THE GODS LIKE TO INVOLVE THEMSELVES IN ALL SORTS OF MATTERS THAT SHOULDN'T CONCERN THEM, AS YOU WELL KNOW.
IT IS A VERY SMALL NUMBER OF MORTALS WHO CAN FIND GLORY IN BATTLE WITHOUT UNKNOWINGLY KILLING THE FAVORITE OF SOME GOD, OR OTHERWISE EARNING THE ENMITY OF SOME DIETY.
MIGHT AS WELL MAKE ELYSIUM A HAVEN FOR MORTALS WHO DIE BY BEING STRUCK BY LIGHTNING.
IT WOULD END UP HAVING ABOUT THE SAME NUMBER OF SHADES AS NOW.

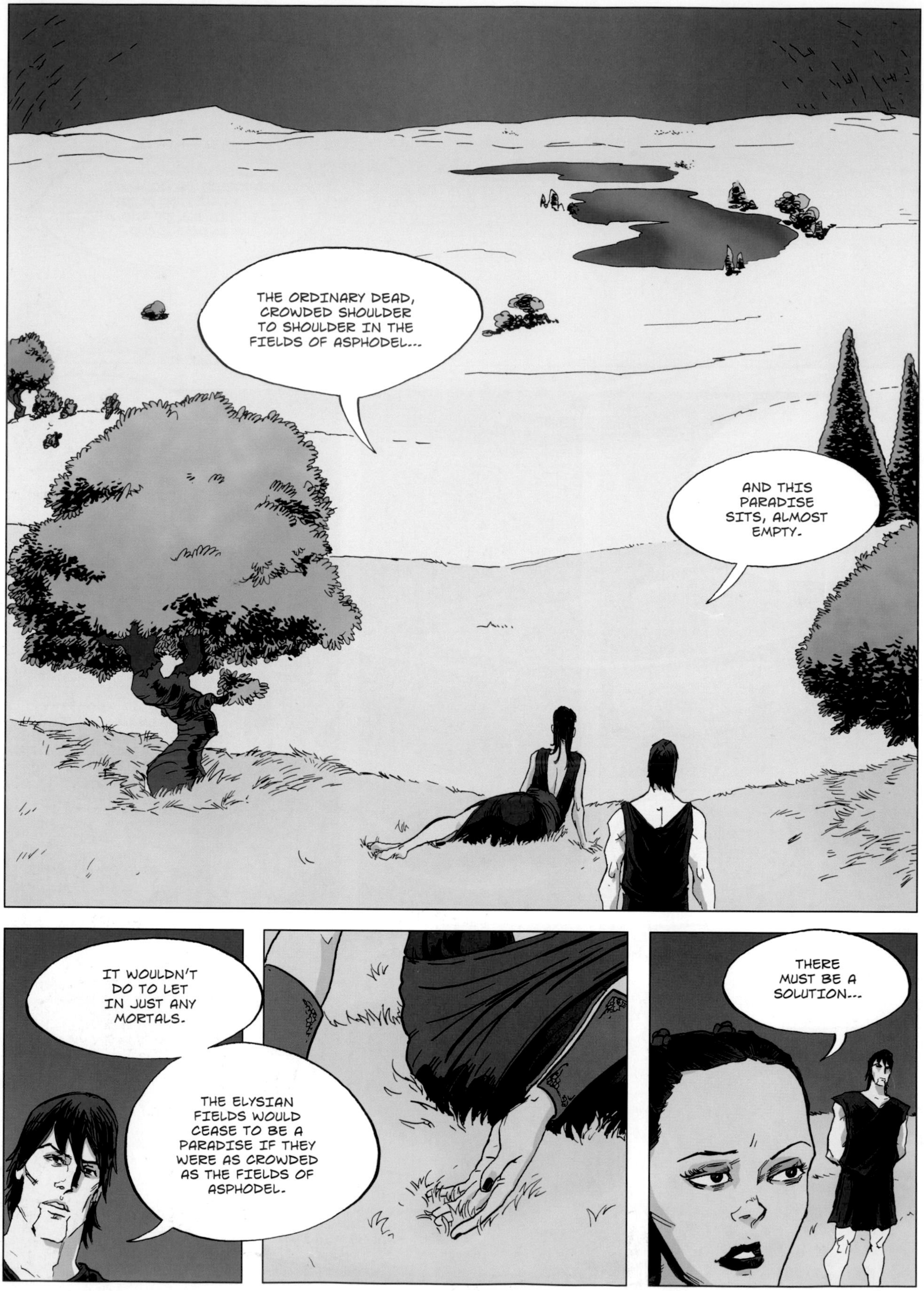
THE ORDINARY DEAD, CROWDED SHOULDER TO SHOULDER IN THE FIELDS OF ASPHODEL...
AND THIS PARADISE SITS, ALMOST EMPTY.
IT WOULDN'T DO TO LET IN JUST ANY MORTALS.
THE ELYSIAN FIELDS WOULD CEASE TO BE A PARADISE IF THEY WERE AS CROWDED AS THE FIELDS OF ASPHODEL.
THERE MUST BE A SOLUTION...

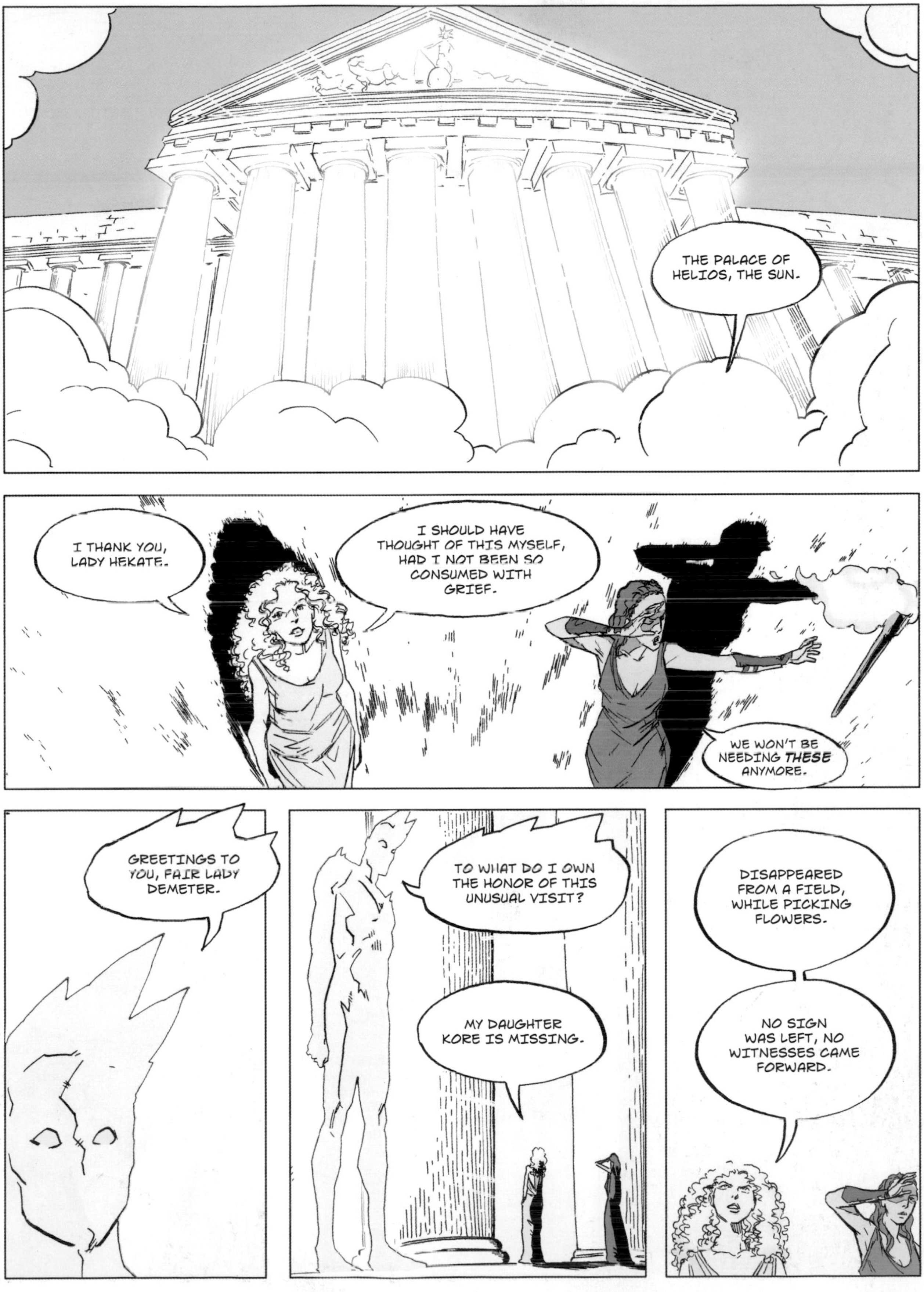
THE PALACE OF HELIOS, THE SUN.
I THANK YOU, LADY HEKATE.
I SHOULD HAVE THOUGHT OF THIS MYSELF, HAD I NOT BEEN SO CONSUMED WITH GRIEF.
WE WON'T BE NEEDING THESE ANYMORE.
GREETINGS TO YOU, FAIR LADY DEMETER.
TO WHAT DO I OWN THE HONOR OF THIS UNUSUAL VISIT?
MY DAUGHTER KORE IS MISSING.
DISAPPEARED FROM A FIELD, WHILE PICKING FLOWERS.
NO SIGN WAS LEFT, NO WITNESSES CAME FORWARD.

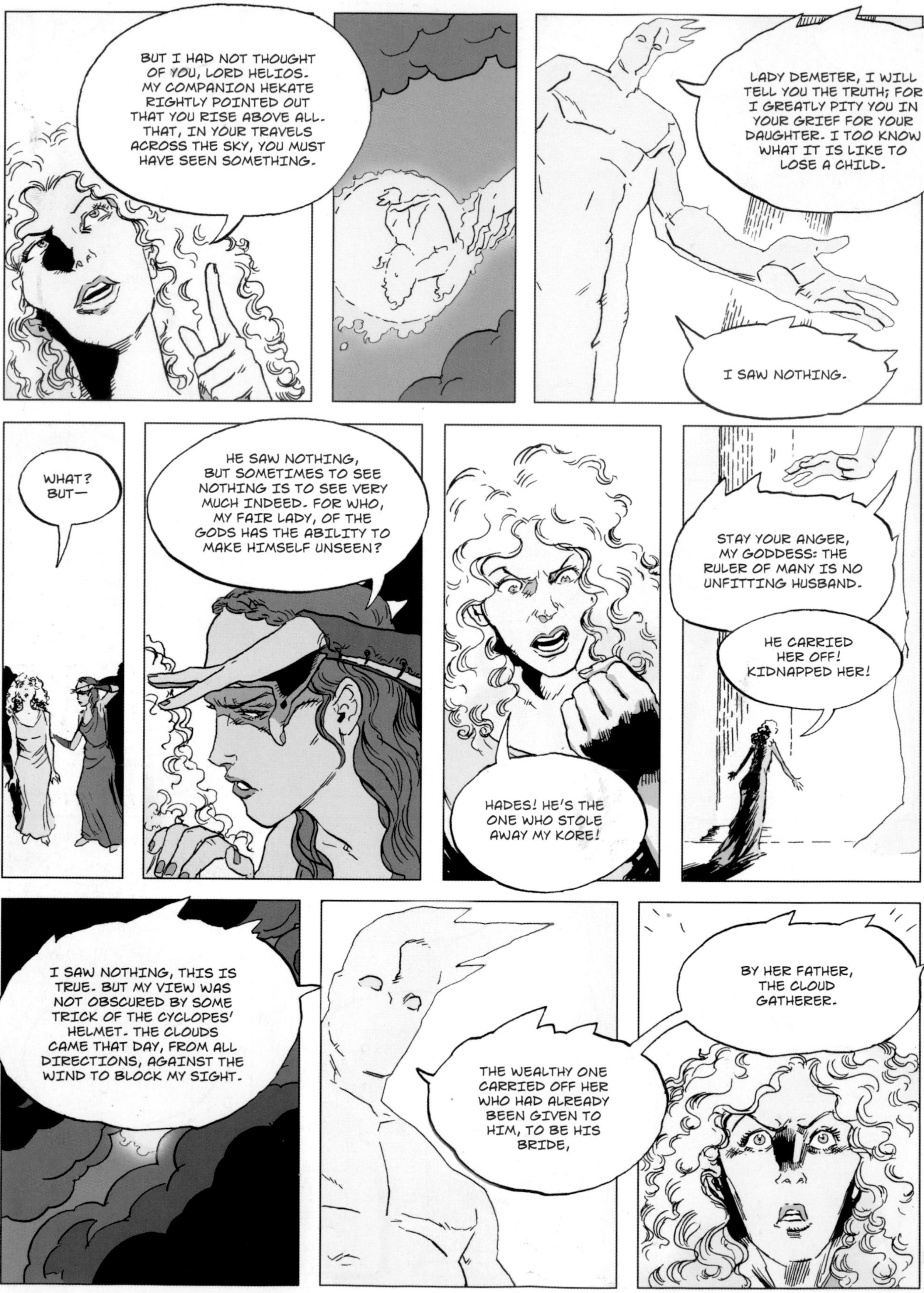
BUT I HAD NOT THOUGHT OF YOU, LORD HELIOS. MY COMPANION HEKATE RIGHTLY POINTED OUT THAT YOU RISE ABOVE ALL. THAT, IN YOUR TRAVELS ACROSS THE SKY, YOU MUST HAVE SEEN SOMETHING.
LADY DEMETER, I WILL TELL YOU THE TRUTH; FOR I GREATLY PITY YOU IN YOUR GRIEF FOR YOUR DAUGHTER. I TOO KNOW WHAT IT IS LIKE TO LOSE A CHILD.
I SAW NOTHING.
WHAT? BUT—
HE SAW NOTHING, BUT SOMETIMES TO SEE NOTHING IS TO SEE VERY MUCH INDEED. FOR WHO, MY FAIR LADY, OF THE GODS HAS THE ABILITY TO MAKE HIMSELF UNSEEN?
HADES! HE'S THE ONE WHO STOLE AWAY MY KORE!
STAY YOUR ANGER, MY GODDESS: THE RULER OF MANY IS NO UNFITTING HUSBAND.
HE CARRIED HER OFF! KIDNAPPED HER!
I SAW NOTHING, THIS IS TRUE. BUT MY VIEW WAS NOT OBSCURED BY SOME TRICK OF THE CYCLOPES' HELMET. THE CLOUDS CAME THAT DAY, FROM ALL DIRECTIONS, AGAINST THE WIND TO BLOCK MY SIGHT.
THE WEALTHY ONE CARRIED OFF HER WHO HAD ALREADY BEEN GIVEN TO HIM, TO BE HIS BRIDE,
BY HER FATHER, THE CLOUD GATHERER.

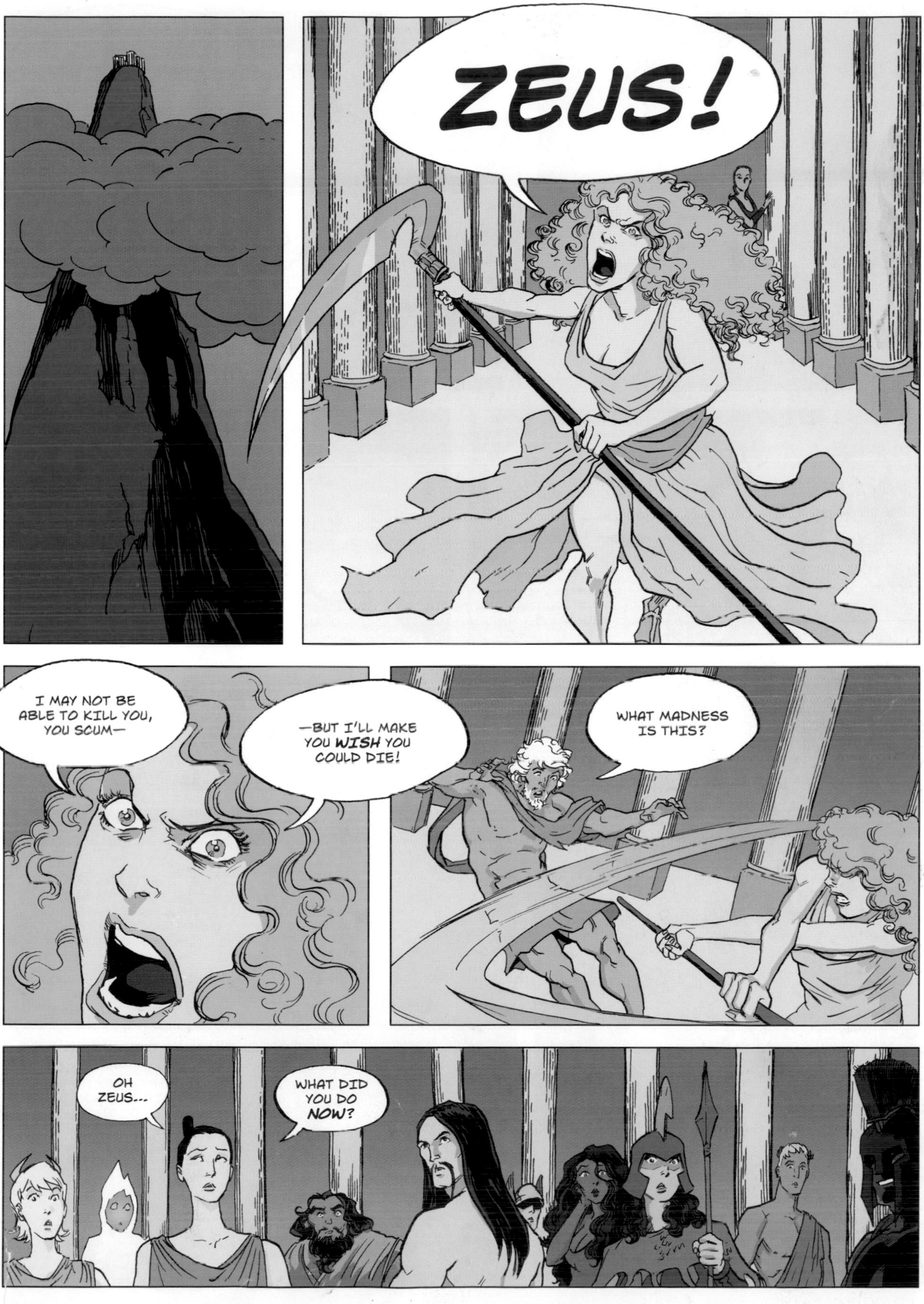
ZEUS!
I MAY NOT BE ABLE TO KILL YOU, YOU SCUM—
—BUT I'LL MAKE YOU WISH YOU COULD DIE!
WHAT MADNESS IS THIS?
OH ZEUS...
WHAT DID YOU DO NOW?

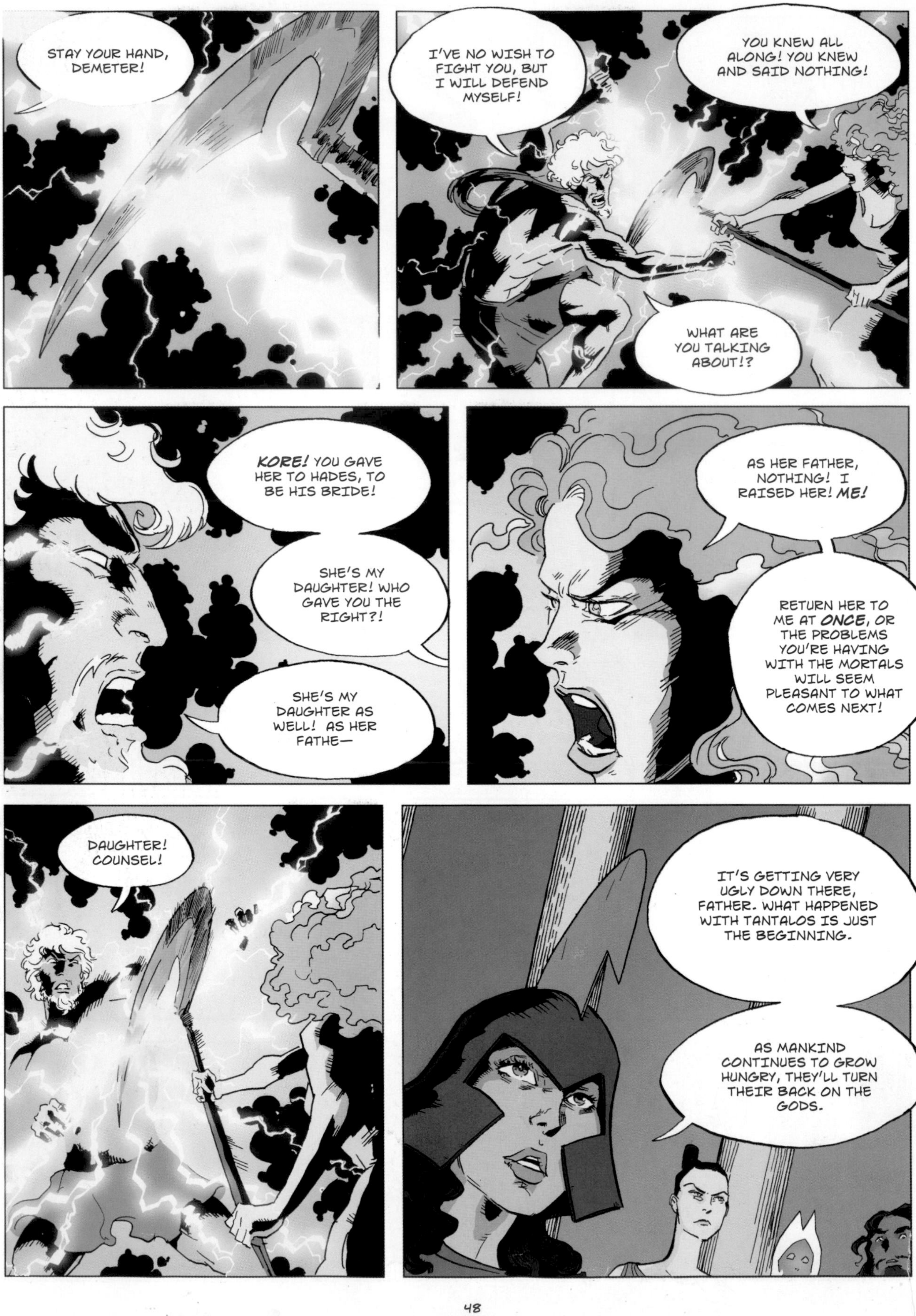
STAY YOUR HAND, DEMETER!
I'VE NO WISH TO FIGHT YOU, BUT I WILL DEFEND MYSELF!
YOU KNEW ALL ALONG! YOU KNEW AND SAID NOTHING!
WHAT ARE YOU TALKING ABOUT!?
KORE! YOU GAVE HER TO HADES, TO BE HIS BRIDE!
SHE'S MY DAUGHTER! WHO GAVE YOU THE RIGHT?!
SHE'S MY DAUGHTER AS WELL! AS HER FATHE—
AS HER FATHER, NOTHING! I RAISED HER! ME!
RETURN HER TO ME AT ONCE, OR THE PROBLEMS YOU'RE HAVING WITH THE MORTALS WILL SEEM PLEASANT TO WHAT COMES NEXT!
DAUGHTER! COUNSEL!
IT'S GETTING VERY UGLY DOWN THERE, FATHER. WHAT HAPPENED WITH TANTALOS IS JUST THE BEGINNING.
AS MANKIND CONTINUES TO GROW HUNGRY, THEY'LL TURN THEIR BACK ON THE GODS.

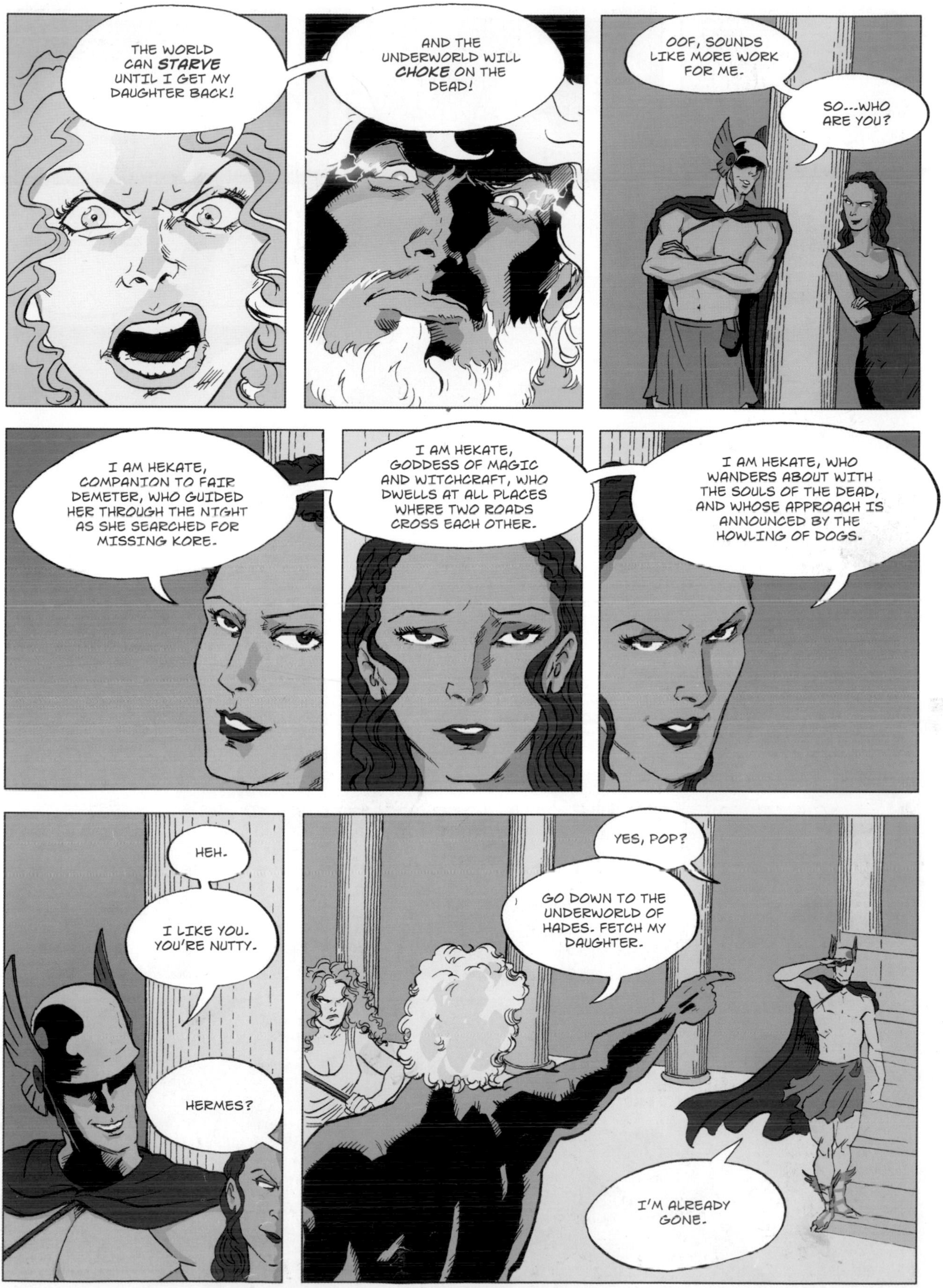
THE WORLD CAN STARVE UNTIL I GET MY DAUGHTER BACK!
AND THE UNDERWORLD WILL CHOKE ON THE DEAD!
OOF, SOUNDS LIKE MORE WORK FOR ME.
SO...WHO ARE YOU?
I AM HEKATE, COMPANION TO FAIR DEMETER, WHO GUIDED HER THROUGH THE NIGHT AS SHE SEARCHED FOR MISSING KORE.
I AM HEKATE, GODDESS OF MAGIC AND WITCHCRAFT, WHO DWELLS AT ALL PLACES WHERE TWO ROADS CROSS EACH OTHER.
I AM HEKATE, WHO WANDERS ABOUT WITH THE SOULS OF THE DEAD, AND WHOSE APPROACH IS ANNOUNCED BY THE HOWLING OF DOGS.
HEH.
I LIKE YOU. YOU'RE NUTTY.
HERMES?
YES, POP?
GO DOWN TO THE UNDERWORLD OF HADES. FETCH MY DAUGHTER.
I'M ALREADY GONE.

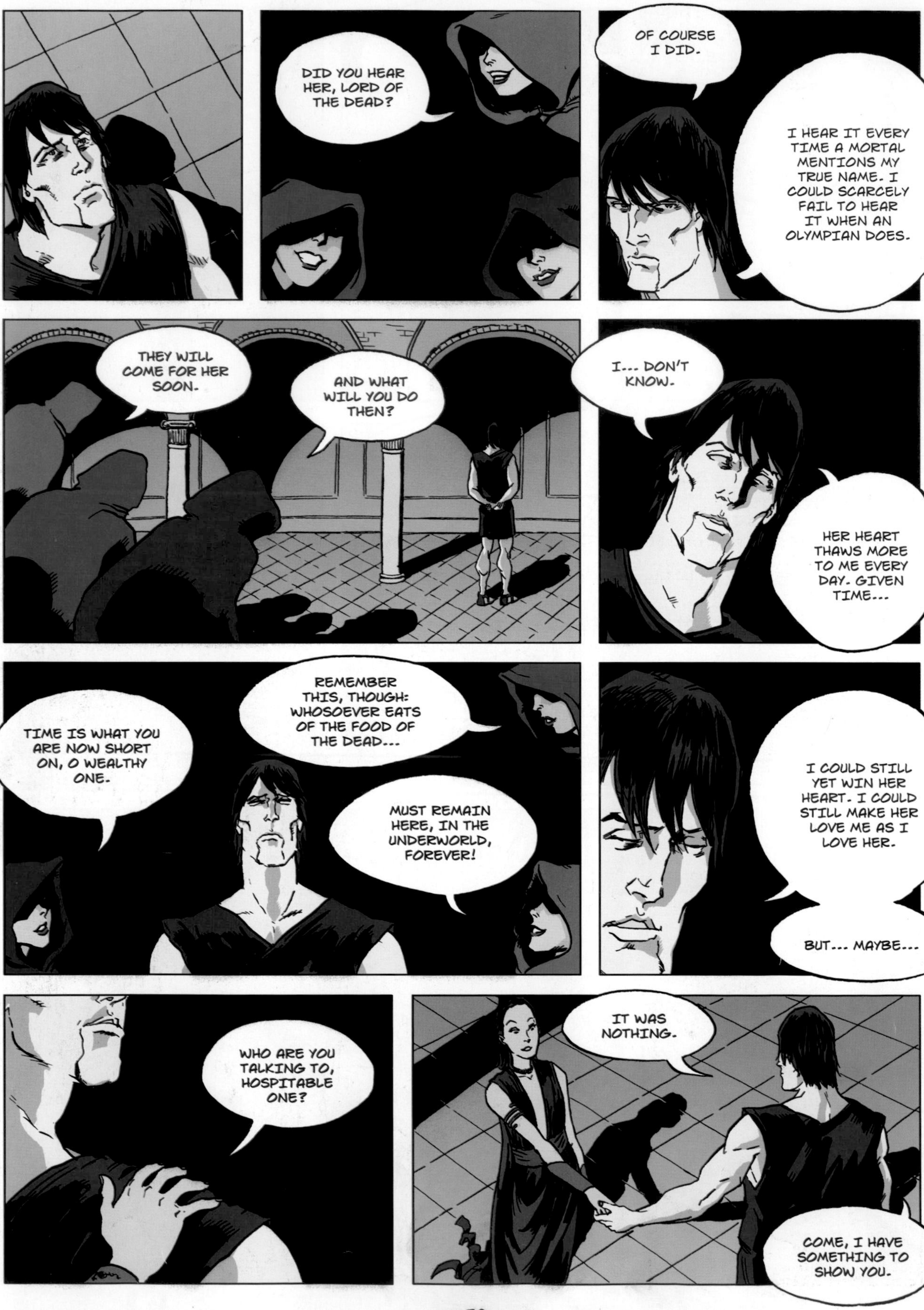
DID YOU HEAR HER, LORD OF THE DEAD?
OF COURSE I DID.
I HEAR IT EVERY TIME A MORTAL MENTIONS MY TRUE NAME. I COULD SCARCELY FAIL TO HEAR IT WHEN AN OLYMPIAN DOES.
THEY WILL COME FOR HER SOON.
AND WHAT WILL YOU DO THEN?
I... DON'T KNOW.
HER HEART THAWS MORE TO ME EVERY DAY. GIVEN TIME...
TIME IS WHAT YOU ARE NOW SHORT ON, O WEALTHY ONE.
REMEMBER THIS, THOUGH: WHOSOEVER EATS OF THE FOOD OF THE DEAD...
MUST REMAIN HERE, IN THE UNDERWORLD, FOREVER!
I COULD STILL YET WIN HER HEART. I COULD STILL MAKE HER LOVE ME AS I LOVE HER.
BUT... MAYBE...
WHO ARE YOU TALKING TO, HOSPITABLE ONE?
IT WAS NOTHING.
COME, I HAVE SOMETHING TO SHOW YOU.

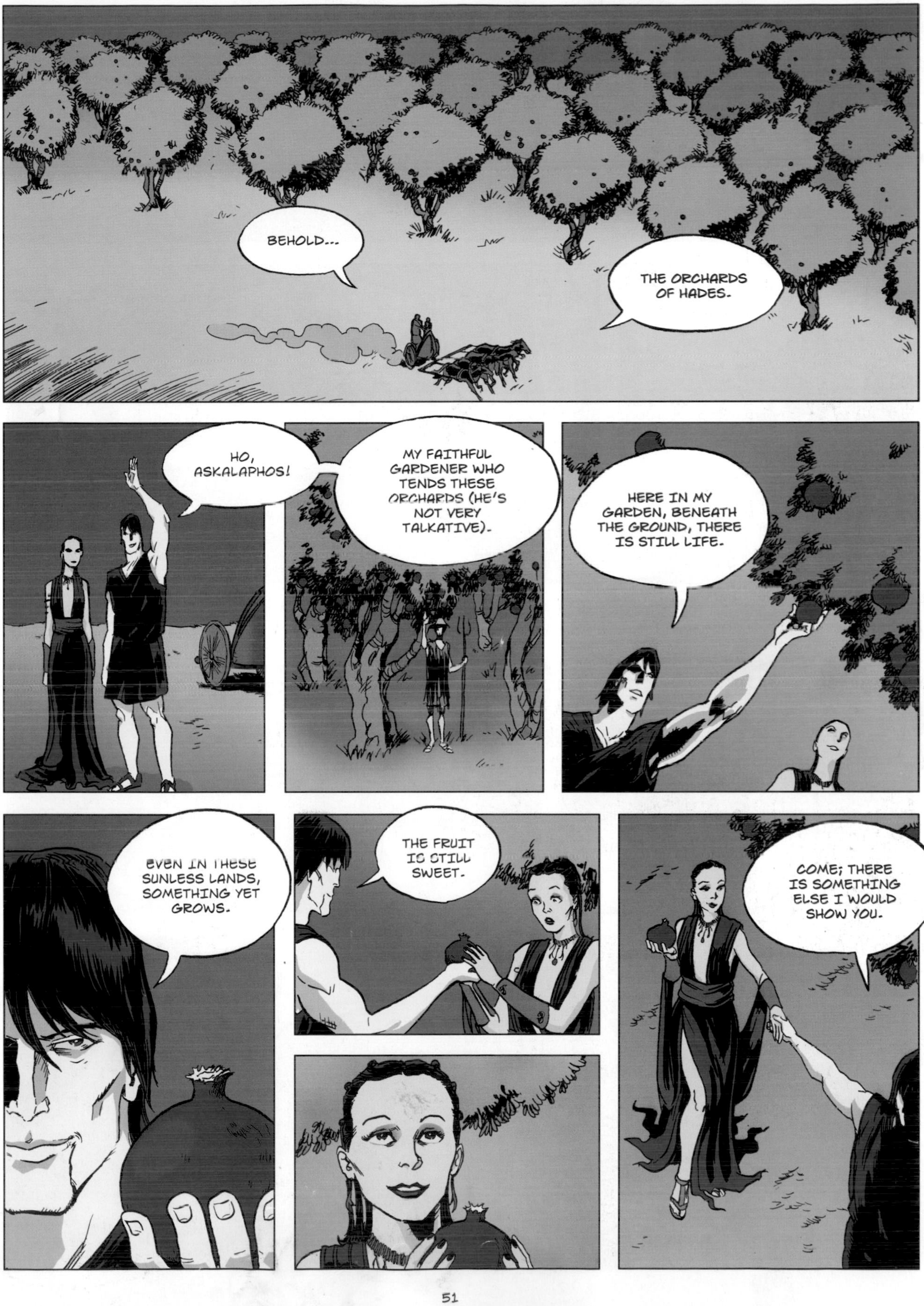

BEHOLD...
THE ORCHARDS OF HADES.
HO, ASKALAPHOS!
MY FAITHFUL GARDENER WHO TENDS THESE ORCHARDS (HE'S NOT VERY TALKATIVE).
HERE IN MY GARDEN, BENEATH THE GROUND, THERE IS STILL LIFE.
EVEN IN THESE SUNLESS LANDS, SOMETHING YET GROWS.
THE FRUIT IS STILL SWEET.
COME; THERE IS SOMETHING ELSE I WOULD SHOW YOU.

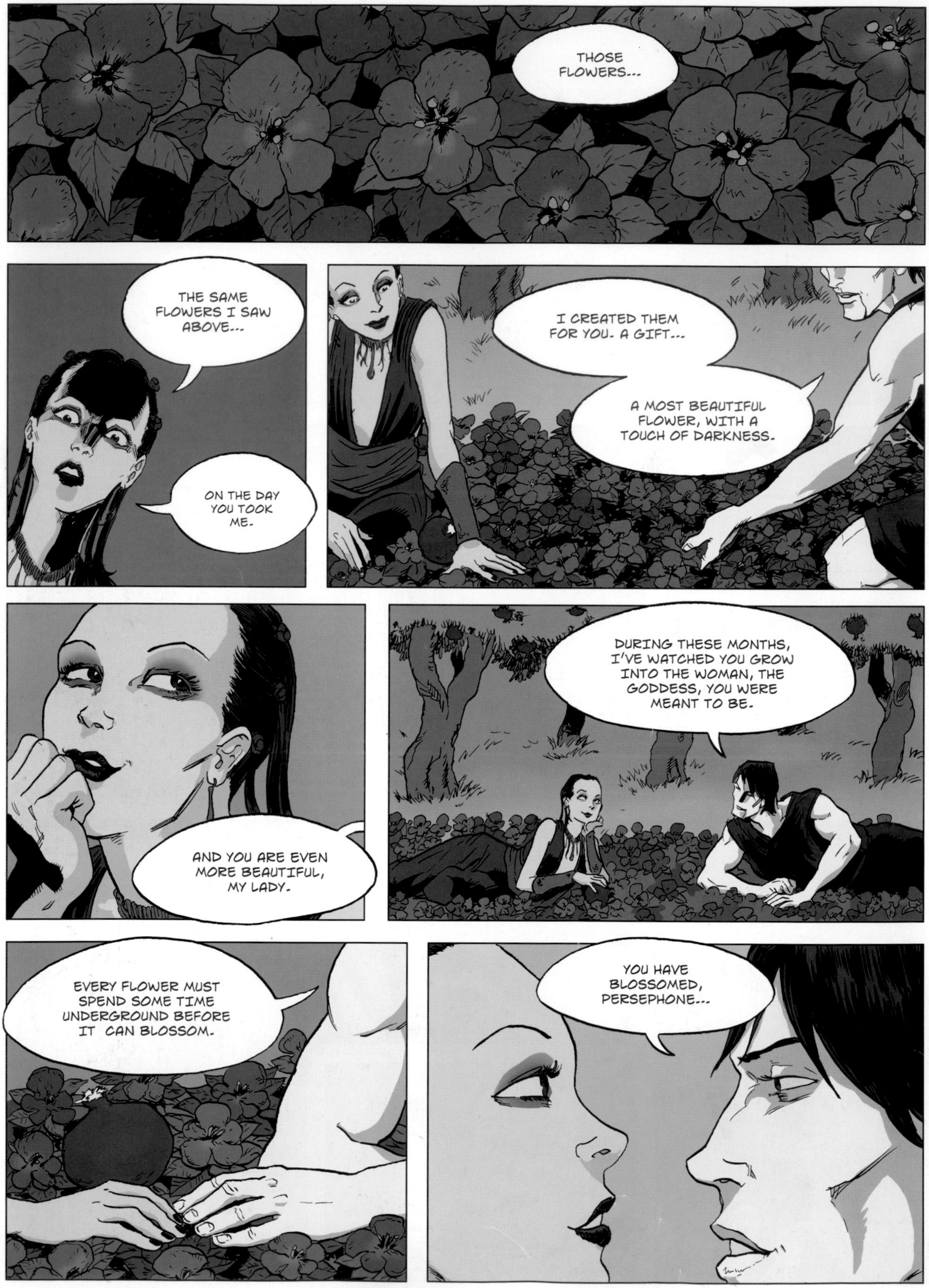
THOSE FLOWERS...
THE SAME FLOWERS I SAW ABOVE...
ON THE DAY YOU TOOK ME.
I CREATED THEM FOR YOU. A GIFT...
A MOST BEAUTIFUL FLOWER, WITH A TOUCH OF DARKNESS.
AND YOU ARE EVEN MORE BEAUTIFUL, MY LADY.
DURING THESE MONTHS, I'VE WATCHED YOU GROW INTO THE WOMAN, THE GODDESS, YOU WERE MEANT TO BE.
EVERY FLOWER MUST SPEND SOME TIME UNDERGROUND BEFORE IT CAN BLOSSOM.
YOU HAVE BLOSSOMED, PERSEPHONE...

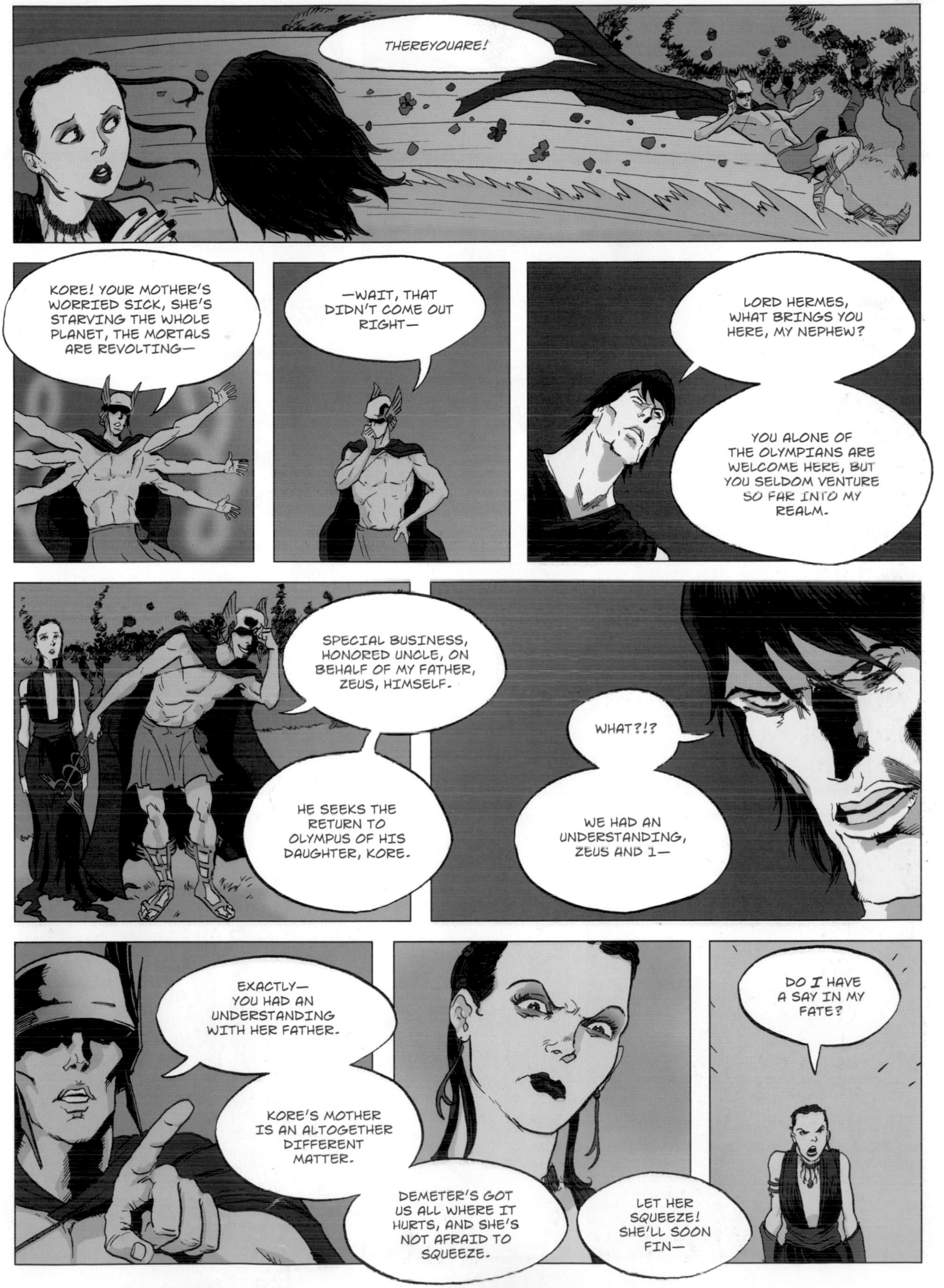
THEREYOUARE!
KORE! YOUR MOTHER'S WORRIED SICK, SHE'S STARVING THE WHOLE PLANET, THE MORTALS ARE REVOLTING—
—WAIT, THAT DIDN'T COME OUT RIGHT—
LORD HERMES, WHAT BRINGS YOU HERE, MY NEPHEW?
YOU ALONE OF THE OLYMPIANS ARE WELCOME HERE, BUT YOU SELDOM VENTURE SO FAR INTO MY REALM.
SPECIAL BUSINESS, HONORED UNCLE, ON BEHALF OF MY FATHER, ZEUS, HIMSELF.
HE SEEKS THE RETURN TO OLYMPUS OF HIS DAUGHTER, KORE.
WHAT?!?
WE HAD AN UNDERSTANDING, ZEUS AND I—
EXACTLY— YOU HAD AN UNDERSTANDING WITH HER FATHER.
KORE'S MOTHER IS AN ALTOGETHER DIFFERENT MATTER.
DEMETER'S GOT US ALL WHERE IT HURTS, AND SHE'S NOT AFRAID TO SQUEEZE.
LET HER SQUEEZE! SHE'LL SOON FIN—
DO I HAVE A SAY IN MY FATE?

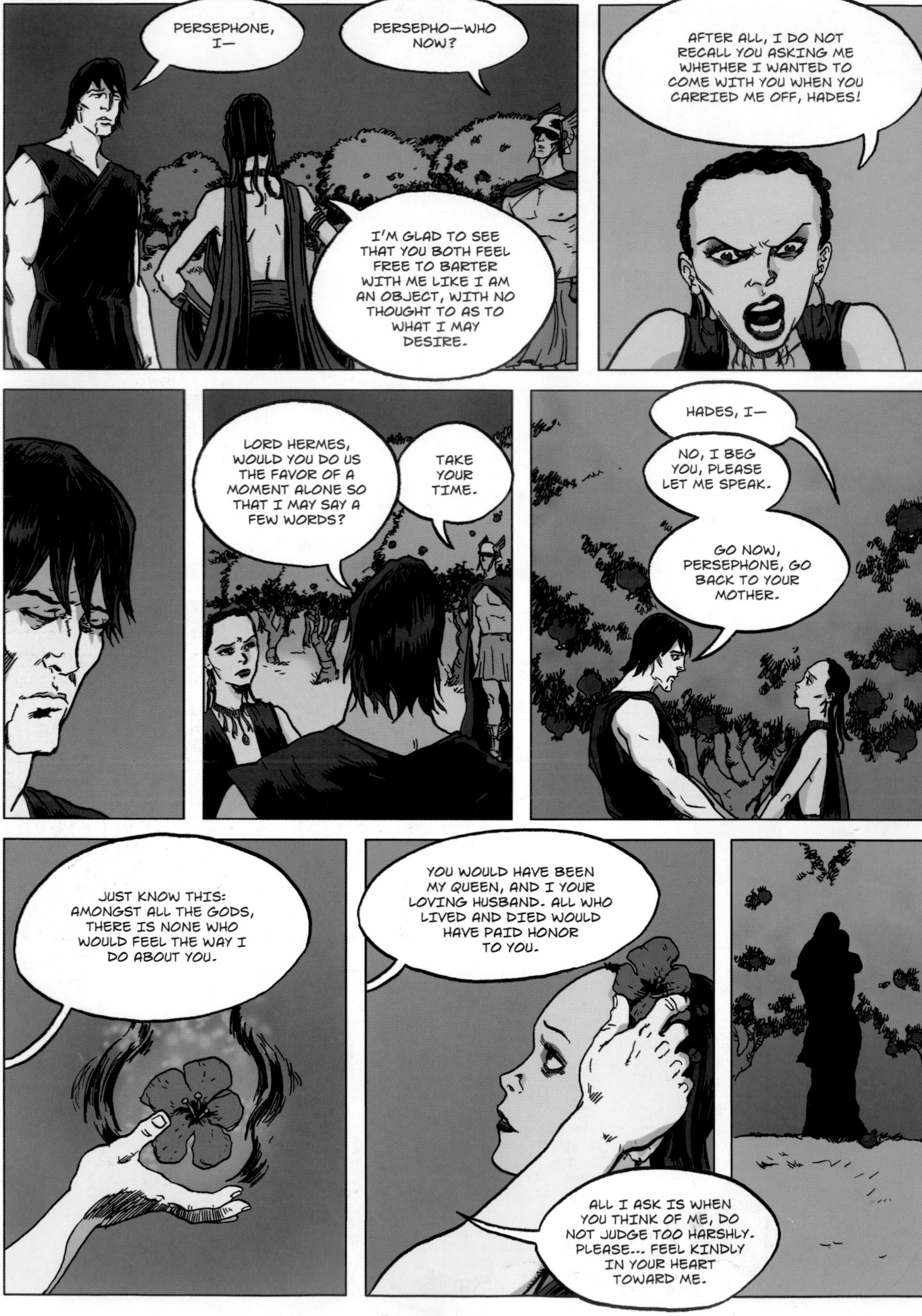
PERSEPHONE, I—
PERSEPHO—WHO NOW?
I'M GLAD TO SEE THAT YOU BOTH FEEL FREE TO BARTER WITH ME LIKE I AM AN OBJECT, WITH NO THOUGHT TO AS TO WHAT I MAY DESIRE.
AFTER ALL, I DO NOT RECALL YOU ASKING ME WHETHER I WANTED TO COME WITH YOU WHEN YOU CARRIED ME OFF, HADES!
LORD HERMES, WOULD YOU DO US THE FAVOR OF A MOMENT ALONE SO THAT I MAY SAY A FEW WORDS?
TAKE YOUR TIME.
HADES, I—
NO, I BEG YOU, PLEASE LET ME SPEAK.
GO NOW, PERSEPHONE, GO BACK TO YOUR MOTHER.
JUST KNOW THIS: AMONGST ALL THE GODS, THERE IS NONE WHO WOULD FEEL THE WAY I DO ABOUT YOU.
YOU WOULD HAVE BEEN MY QUEEN, AND I YOUR LOVING HUSBAND. ALL WHO LIVED AND DIED WOULD HAVE PAID HONOR TO YOU.
ALL I ASK IS WHEN YOU THINK OF ME, DO NOT JUDGE TOO HARSHLY. PLEASE... FEEL KINDLY IN YOUR HEART TOWARD ME.

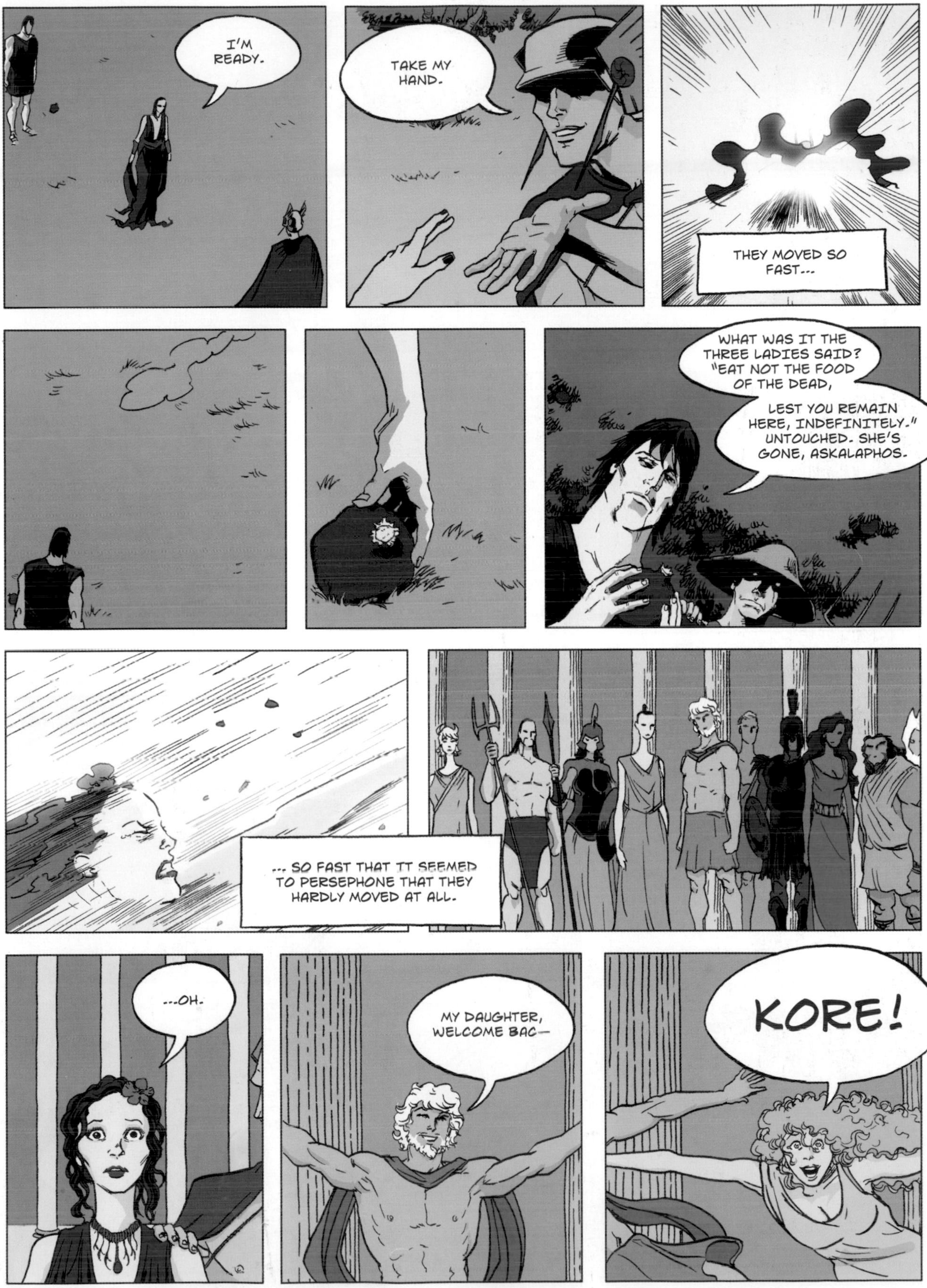

I'M READY.
TAKE MY HAND.
THEY MOVED SO FAST...
WHAT WAS IT THE THREE LADIES SAID? "EAT NOT THE FOOD OF THE DEAD,
LEST YOU REMAIN HERE, INDEFINITELY." UNTOUCHED. SHE'S GONE, ASKALAPHOS.
... SO FAST THAT IT SEEMED TO PERSEPHONE THAT THEY HARDLY MOVED AT ALL.
...OH.
MY DAUGHTER, WELCOME BAC—
KORE!

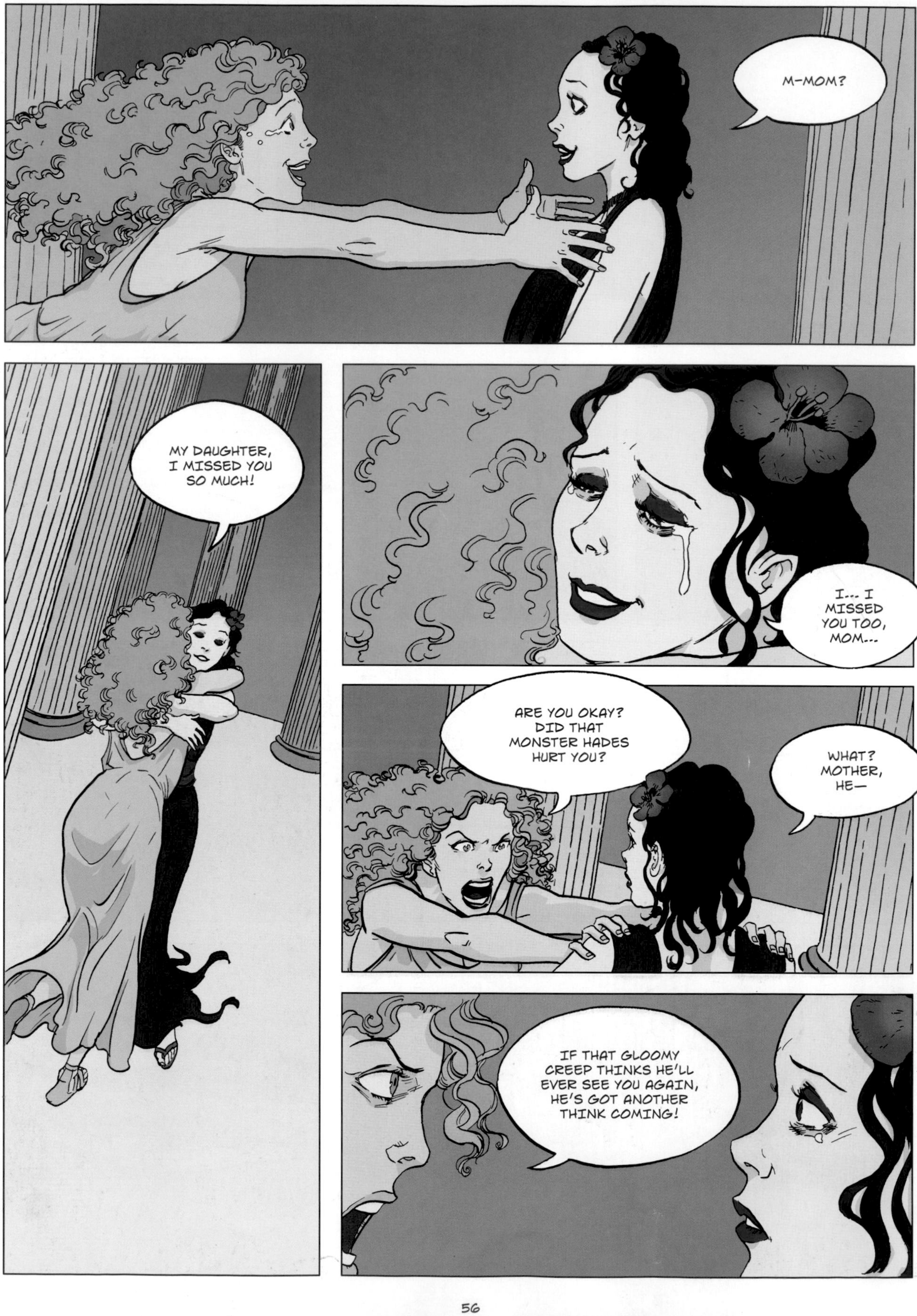
M-MOM?
MY DAUGHTER, I MISSED YOU SO MUCH!
I... I MISSED YOU TOO, MOM...
ARE YOU OKAY? DID THAT MONSTER HADES HURT YOU?
WHAT? MOTHER, HE—
IF THAT GLOOMY CREEP THINKS HE'LL EVER SEE YOU AGAIN, HE'S GOT ANOTHER THINK COMING!

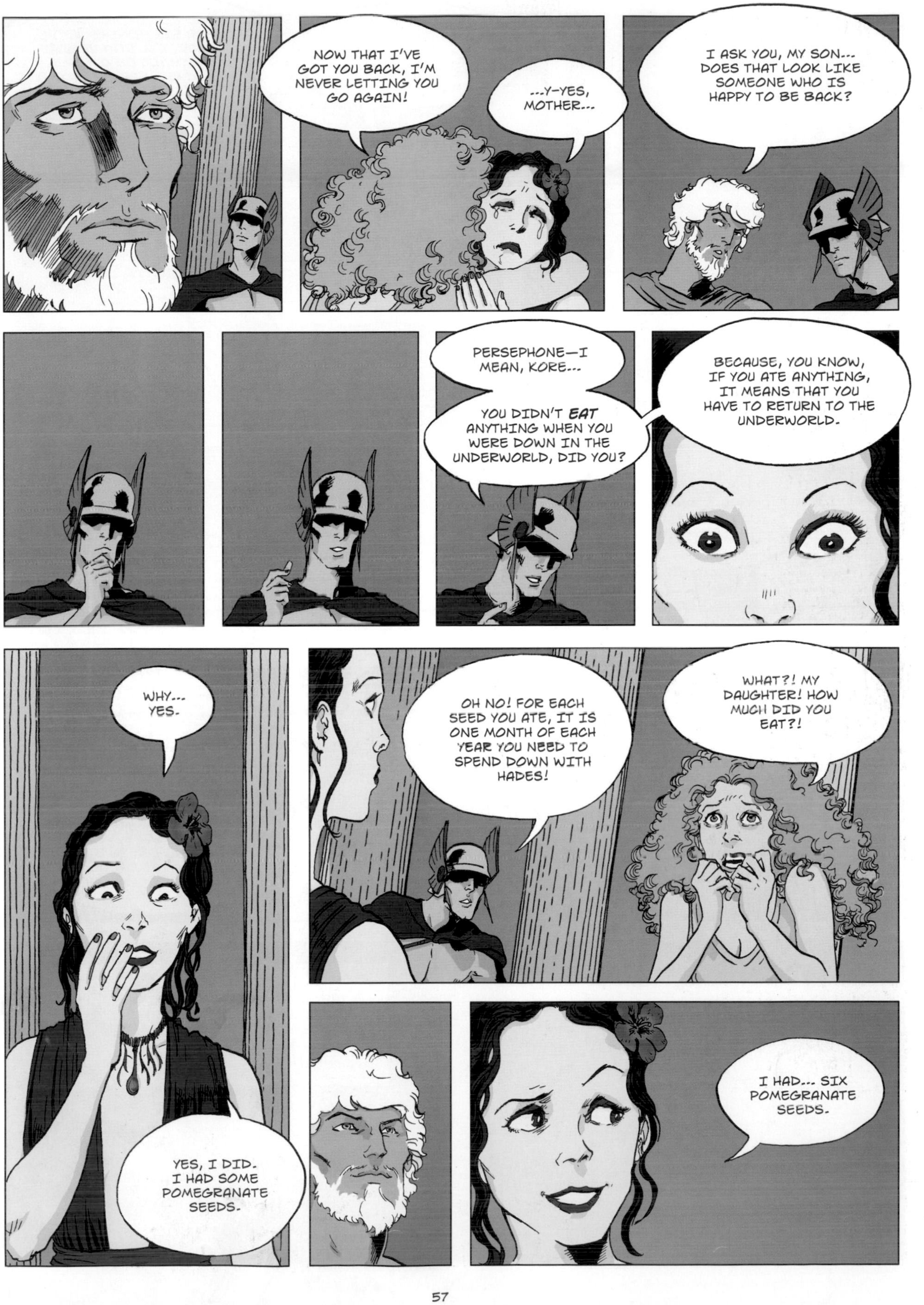
NOW THAT I'VE GOT YOU BACK, I'M NEVER LETTING YOU GO AGAIN!
...Y-YES, MOTHER...
I ASK YOU, MY SON... DOES THAT LOOK LIKE SOMEONE WHO IS HAPPY TO BE BACK?
PERSEPHONE—I MEAN, KORE...
YOU DIDN'T EAT ANYTHING WHEN YOU WERE DOWN IN THE UNDERWORLD, DID YOU?
BECAUSE, YOU KNOW, IF YOU ATE ANYTHING, IT MEANS THAT YOU HAVE TO RETURN TO THE UNDERWORLD.
WHY... YES.
YES, I DID. I HAD SOME POMEGRANATE SEEDS.
OH NO! FOR EACH SEED YOU ATE, IT IS ONE MONTH OF EACH YEAR YOU NEED TO SPEND DOWN WITH HADES!
WHAT?! MY DAUGHTER! HOW MUCH DID YOU EAT?!
I HAD... SIX POMEGRANATE SEEDS.

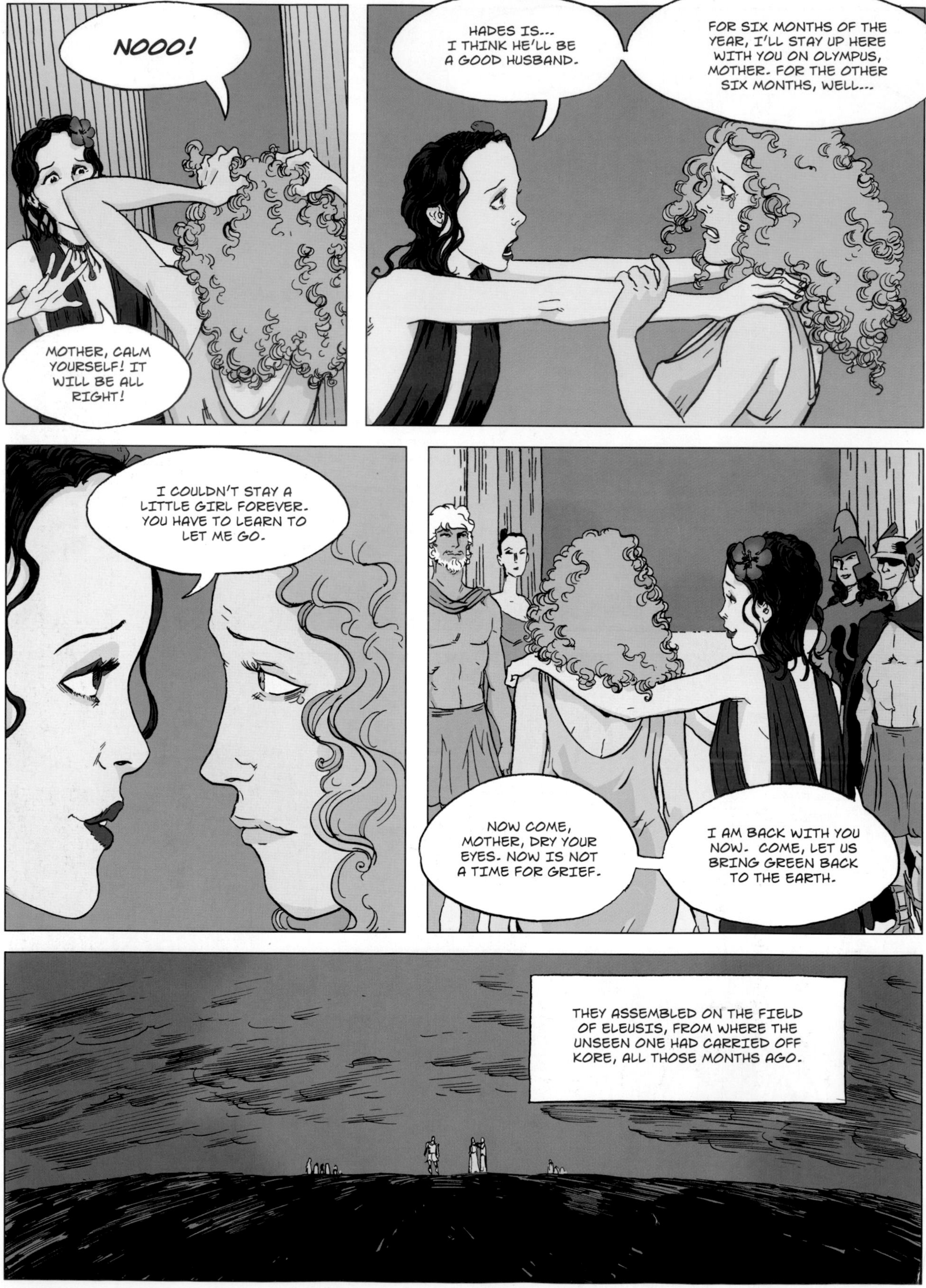
NOOO!
MOTHER, CALM YOURSELF! IT WILL BE ALL RIGHT!
HADES IS... I THINK HE'LL BE A GOOD HUSBAND.
FOR SIX MONTHS OF THE YEAR, I'LL STAY UP HERE WITH YOU ON OLYMPUS, MOTHER. FOR THE OTHER SIX MONTHS, WELL...
I COULDN'T STAY A LITTLE GIRL FOREVER. YOU HAVE TO LEARN TO LET ME GO.
NOW COME, MOTHER, DRY YOUR EYES. NOW IS NOT A TIME FOR GRIEF.
I AM BACK WITH YOU NOW. COME, LET US BRING GREEN BACK TO THE EARTH.
THEY ASSEMBLED ON THE FIELD OF ELEUSIS, FROM WHERE THE UNSEEN ONE HAD CARRIED OFF KORE, ALL THOSE MONTHS AGO.

WITH A WAVE OF HIS HAND, THE KING OF THE GODS SCATTERED THE CLOUDS THAT HAD HIDDEN THE SUN.

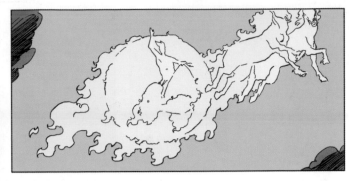

IT'S YOUR TURN NOW, MOTHER...

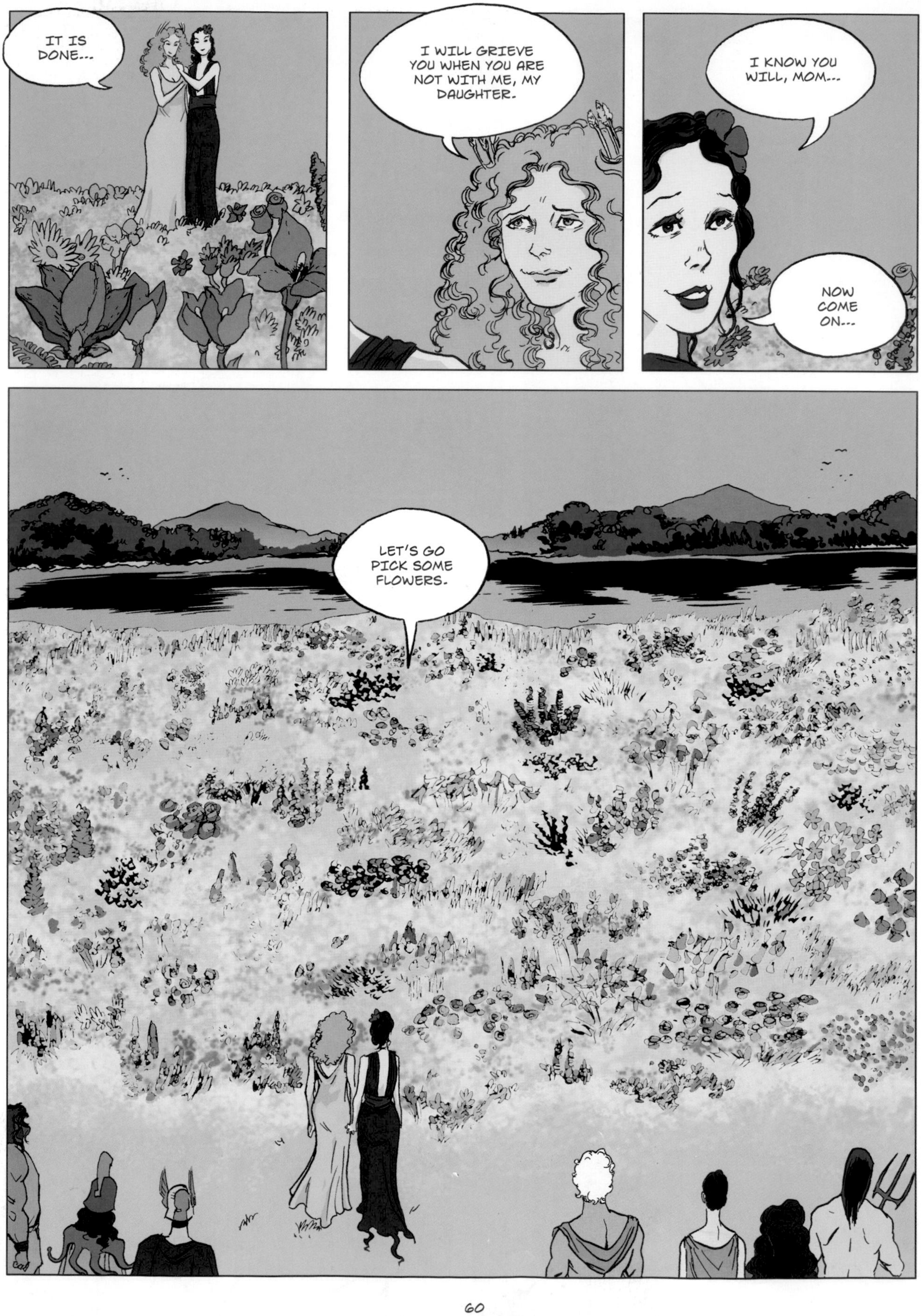
IT IS DONE...
I WILL GRIEVE YOU WHEN YOU ARE NOT WITH ME, MY DAUGHTER.
I KNOW YOU WILL, MOM...
NOW COME ON...
LET'S GO PICK SOME FLOWERS.

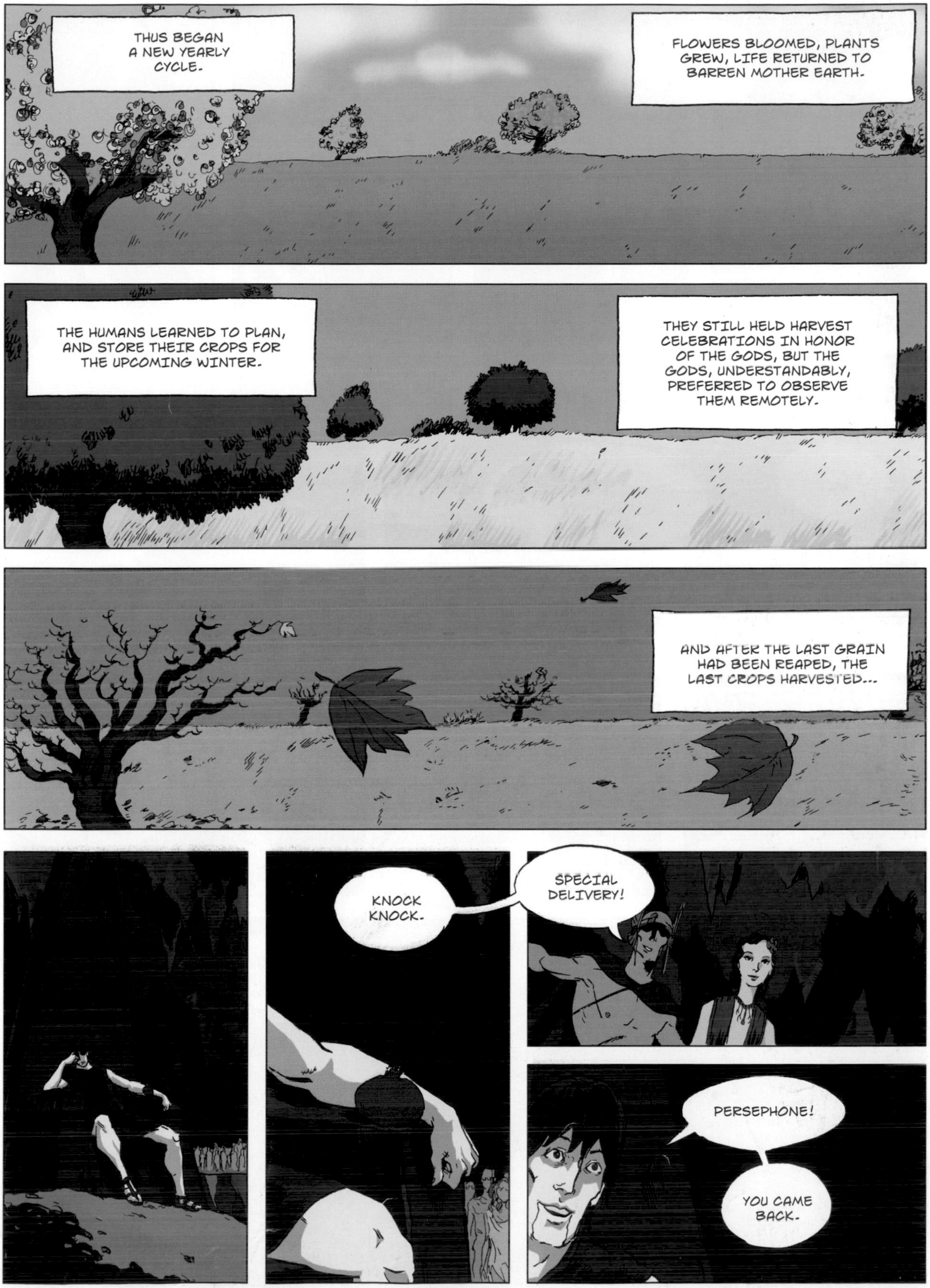
THUS BEGAN A NEW YEARLY CYCLE.
FLOWERS BLOOMED, PLANTS GREW, LIFE RETURNED TO BARREN MOTHER EARTH.
THE HUMANS LEARNED TO PLAN, AND STORE THEIR CROPS FOR THE UPCOMING WINTER.
THEY STILL HELD HARVEST CELEBRATIONS IN HONOR OF THE GODS, BUT THE GODS, UNDERSTANDABLY, PREFERRED TO OBSERVE THEM REMOTELY.
AND AFTER THE LAST GRAIN HAD BEEN REAPED, THE LAST CROPS HARVESTED...
KNOCK KNOCK.
SPECIAL DELIVERY!
PERSEPHONE!
YOU CAME BACK.

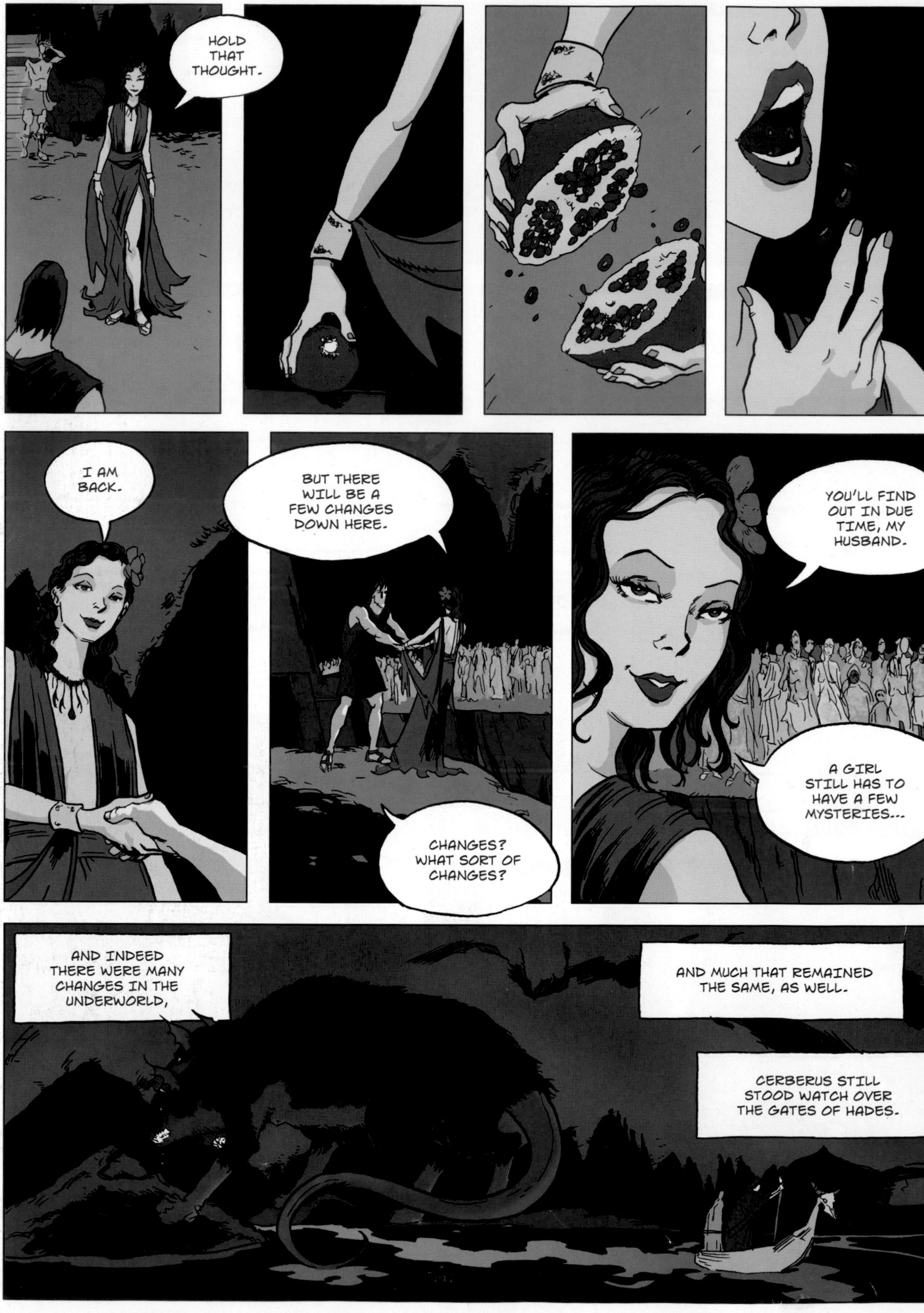
HOLD THAT THOUGHT.
I AM BACK.
BUT THERE WILL BE A FEW CHANGES DOWN HERE.
CHANGES? WHAT SORT OF CHANGES?
YOU'LL FIND OUT IN DUE TIME, MY HUSBAND.
A GIRL STILL HAS TO HAVE A FEW MYSTERIES...
AND INDEED THERE WERE MANY CHANGES IN THE UNDERWORLD,
AND MUCH THAT REMAINED THE SAME, AS WELL.
CERBERUS STILL STOOD WATCH OVER THE GATES OF HADES.

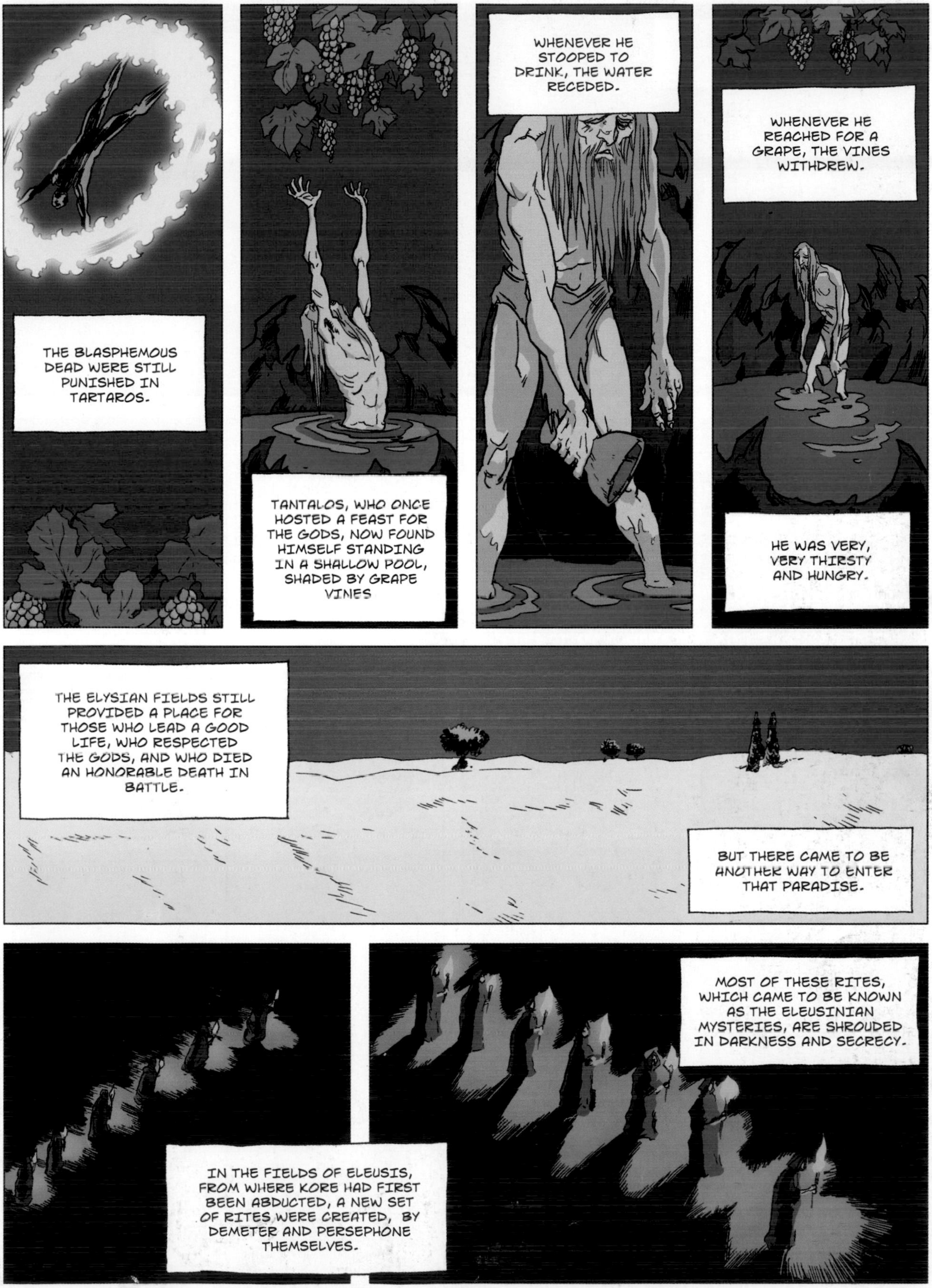
THE BLASPHEMOUS DEAD WERE STILL PUNISHED IN TARTAROS.
TANTALOS, WHO ONCE HOSTED A FEAST FOR THE GODS, NOW FOUND HIMSELF STANDING IN A SHALLOW POOL, SHADED BY GRAPE VINES
WHENEVER HE STOOPED TO DRINK, THE WATER RECEDED.
WHENEVER HE REACHED FOR A GRAPE, THE VINES WITHDREW.
HE WAS VERY, VERY THIRSTY AND HUNGRY.
THE ELYSIAN FIELDS STILL PROVIDED A PLACE FOR THOSE WHO LEAD A GOOD LIFE, WHO RESPECTED THE GODS, AND WHO DIED AN HONORABLE DEATH IN BATTLE.
BUT THERE CAME TO BE ANOTHER WAY TO ENTER THAT PARADISE.
IN THE FIELDS OF ELEUSIS, FROM WHERE KORE HAD FIRST BEEN ABDUCTED, A NEW SET OF RITES WERE CREATED, BY DEMETER AND PERSEPHONE THEMSELVES.
MOST OF THESE RITES, WHICH CAME TO BE KNOWN AS THE ELEUSINIAN MYSTERIES, ARE SHROUDED IN DARKNESS AND SECRECY.

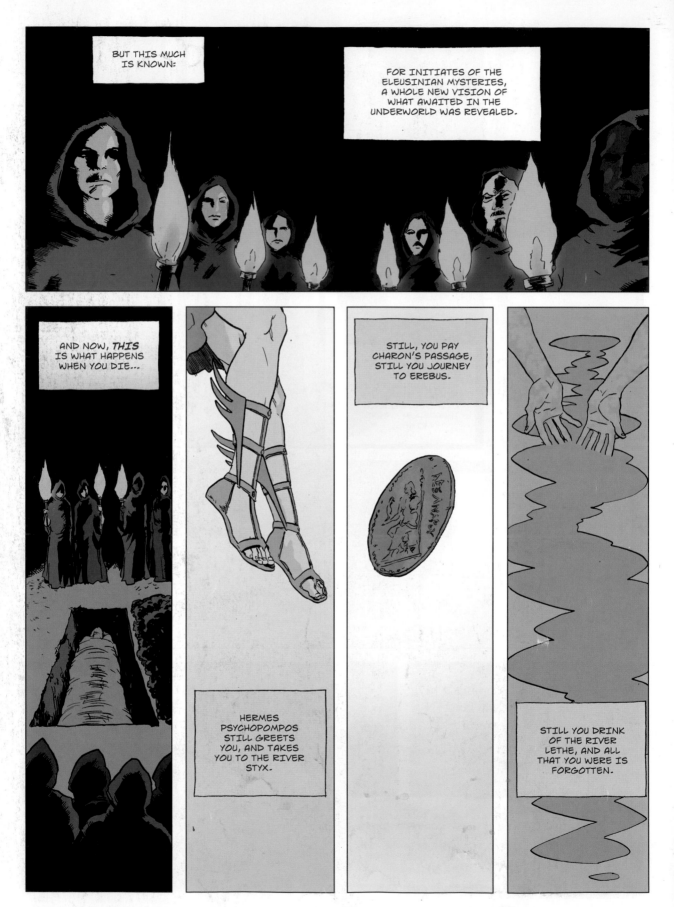

BUT THIS MUCH IS KNOWN:

FOR INITIATES OF THE ELEUSINIAN MYSTERIES, A WHOLE NEW VISION OF WHAT AWAITED IN THE UNDERWORLD WAS REVEALED.

AND NOW, *THIS* IS WHAT HAPPENS WHEN YOU DIE...

STILL, YOU PAY CHARON'S PASSAGE, STILL YOU JOURNEY TO EREBUS.

HERMES PSYCHOPOMPOS STILL GREETS YOU, AND TAKES YOU TO THE RIVER STYX.

STILL YOU DRINK OF THE RIVER LETHE, AND ALL THAT YOU WERE IS FORGOTTEN.

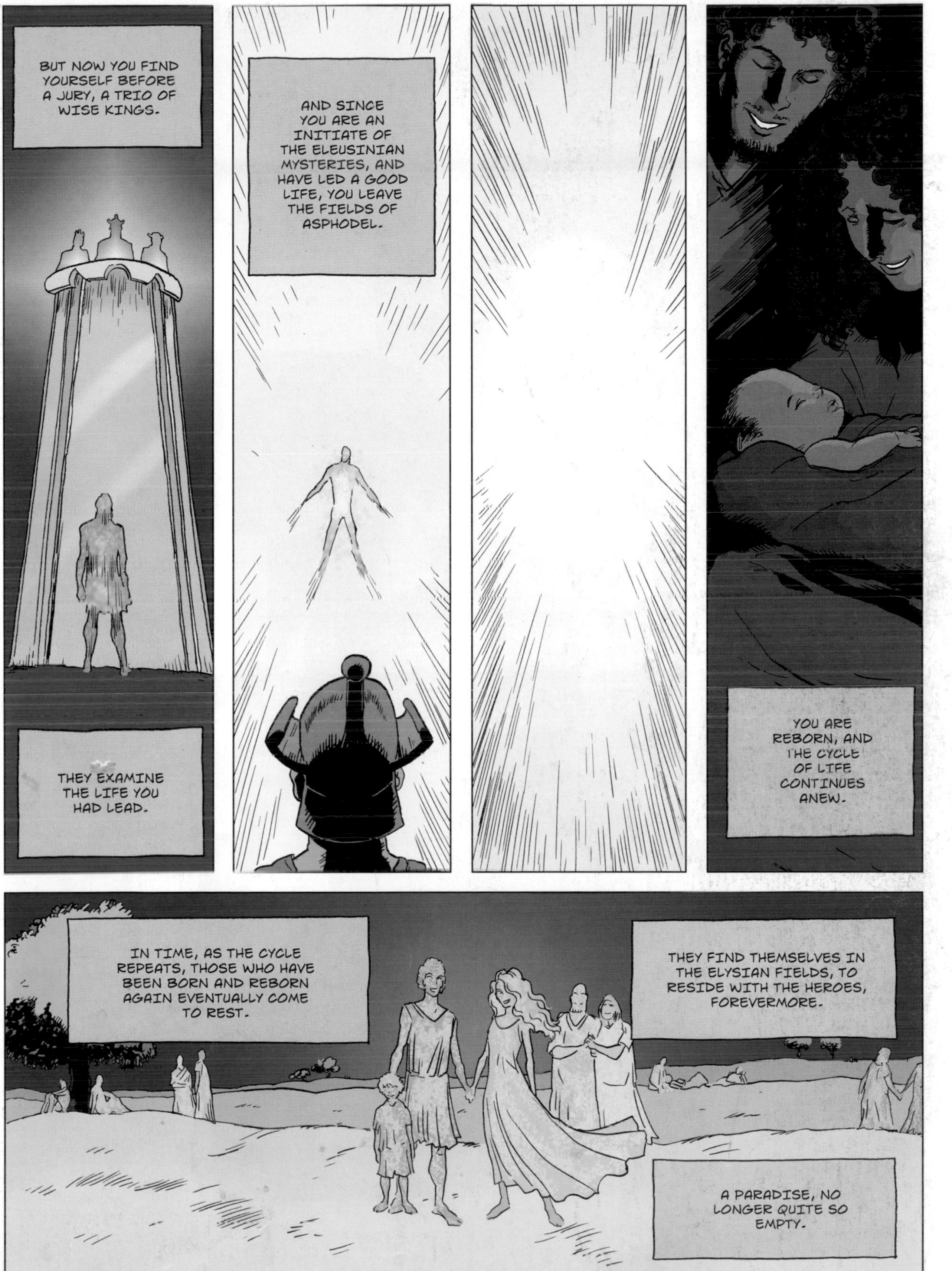
BUT NOW YOU FIND YOURSELF BEFORE A JURY, A TRIO OF WISE KINGS.
THEY EXAMINE THE LIFE YOU HAD LEAD.
AND SINCE YOU ARE AN INITIATE OF THE ELEUSINIAN MYSTERIES, AND HAVE LED A GOOD LIFE, YOU LEAVE THE FIELDS OF ASPHODEL.
YOU ARE REBORN, AND THE CYCLE OF LIFE CONTINUES ANEW.
IN TIME, AS THE CYCLE REPEATS, THOSE WHO HAVE BEEN BORN AND REBORN AGAIN EVENTUALLY COME TO REST.
THEY FIND THEMSELVES IN THE ELYSIAN FIELDS, TO RESIDE WITH THE HEROES, FOREVERMORE.
A PARADISE, NO LONGER QUITE SO EMPTY.

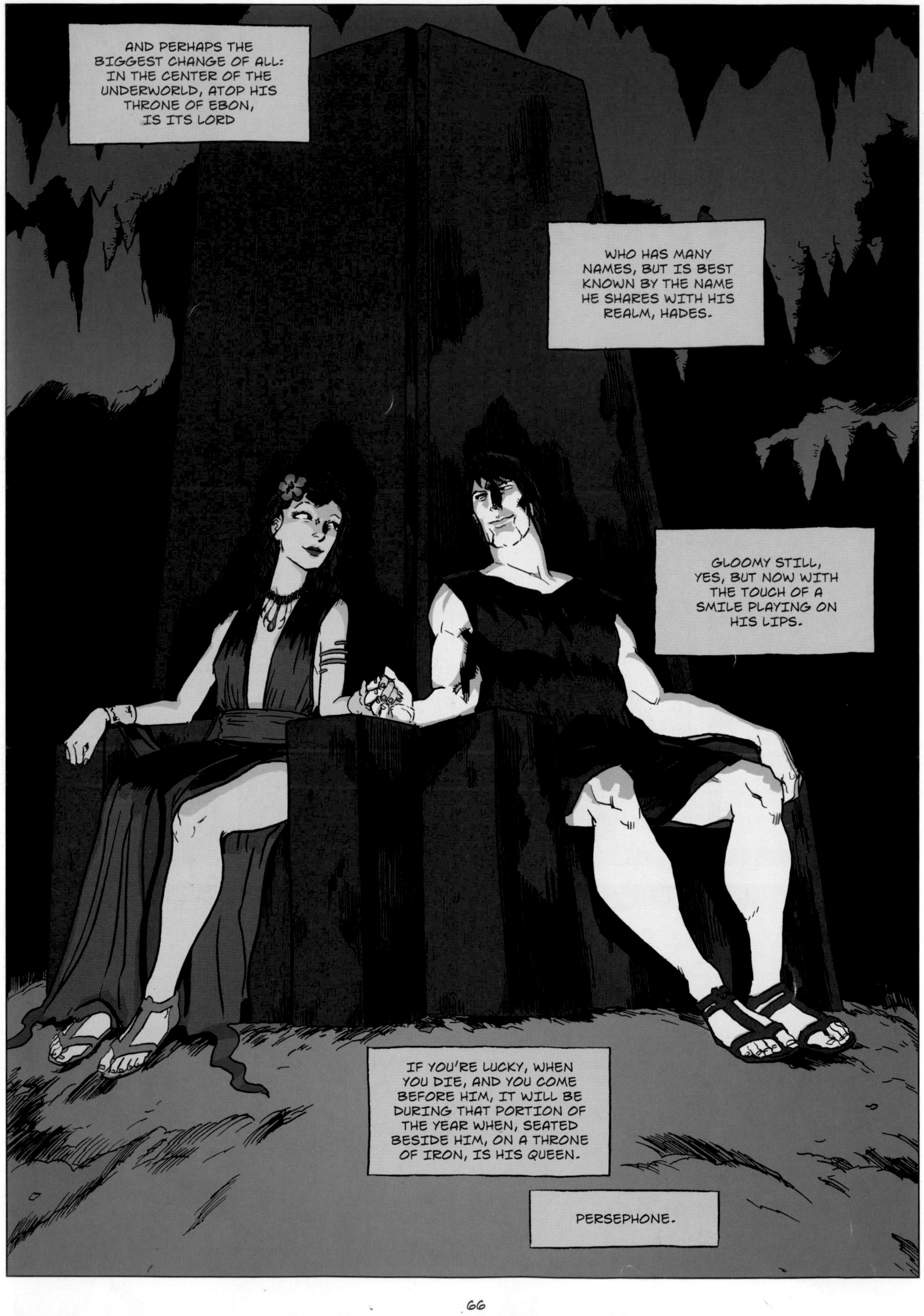
AND PERHAPS THE BIGGEST CHANGE OF ALL: IN THE CENTER OF THE UNDERWORLD, ATOP HIS THRONE OF EBON, IS ITS LORD
WHO HAS MANY NAMES, BUT IS BEST KNOWN BY THE NAME HE SHARES WITH HIS REALM, HADES.
GLOOMY STILL, YES, BUT NOW WITH THE TOUCH OF A SMILE PLAYING ON HIS LIPS.
IF YOU'RE LUCKY, WHEN YOU DIE, AND YOU COME BEFORE HIM, IT WILL BE DURING THAT PORTION OF THE YEAR WHEN, SEATED BESIDE HIM, ON A THRONE OF IRON, IS HIS QUEEN.
PERSEPHONE.

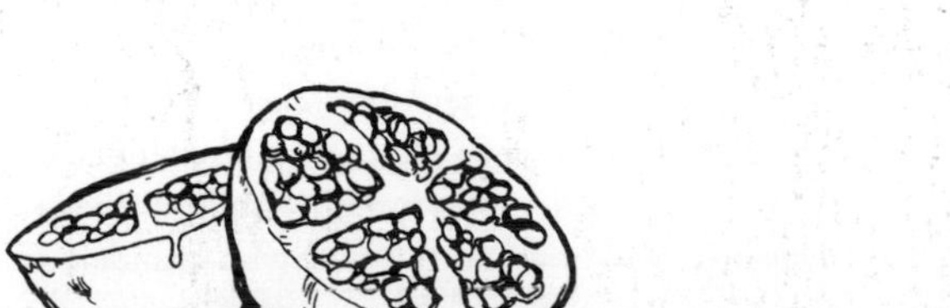

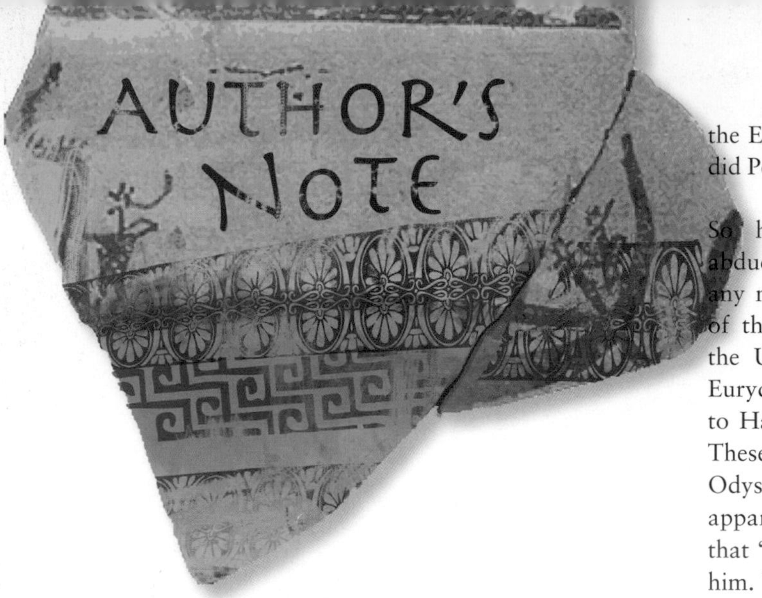
AUTHOR'S
NOTE

First, a confession:

I cheated. Hades is not an Olympian.

Hades is certainly one of the Great Greek Gods, but as far as being a member of the canonical twelve Olympians, well, he's not one, because of his home address. As you've seen in this book, he makes his home deep down in the Underworld. He's joined in this book by Demeter, who is most definitely one of the twelve. But human nature being what it is, readers are going to get more excited about *Hades: Lord of the Dead* than *Demeter: Goddess of the Harvest*.

But honestly? More than Hades, more than Demeter, this book is really about Kore, or Persephone, as she comes to be known. Which is interesting because that's certainly not what I intended when I started writing it. I mean, obviously, she was always going to be a major part—you simply can't tell the story of the Abduction of Persephone without her appearing in a scene or two. But as I read the ancient texts telling of her abduction by Hades (and there are many, many, many ancient texts that tell this story—it's still one of the most popular of all Greek myths), in pretty much every instance, Persephone appears only in exactly that—a scene or two. She appears at the beginning, when she's carried off, and again at the end, when Hermes brings her back. What happened in the middle was all about Demeter, the grieving mother, who wandered the Earth in her daughter's absence. But what did Persephone think about this whole matter?

So here's the interesting part—after the abduction, Persephone never again appears in any myth, in any capacity, but as the Queen of the Dead. When Orpheus goes down to the Underworld to fetch his lost lady-love, Eurydice, Persephone is there, seated next to Hades. When Heracles goes down to free Theseus, Persephone is in attendance. When Odysseus travels to the Underworld, he has no apparent fear of Hades, but he *is* very afraid that "the dread queen Persephone" will notice him. What of her half a year on Olympus? As far as the myths are concerned, we never hear about that.

I've mentioned before how, as a storyteller who is retelling the Greek myths, I'm part of a tradition going back thousands of years. Everyone who has retold this tale before me has added his or her own spin to the proceedings, and now I've added mine as well. And for me that spin was, well, maybe Persephone *likes* being the Queen of the Dead. It would certainly explain why she's apparently always hanging around in the Underworld, and never on Olympus. She seems to have a bit of a dark side.

I wonder how Demeter feels about that?

George O'Connor
Brooklyn, NY
2012

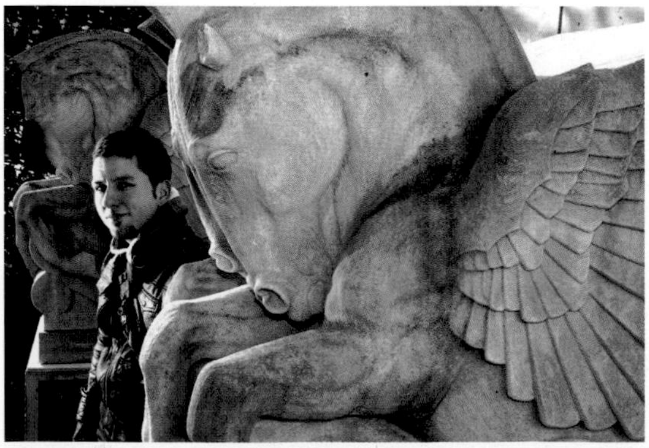

HADES

LORD OF THE DEAD

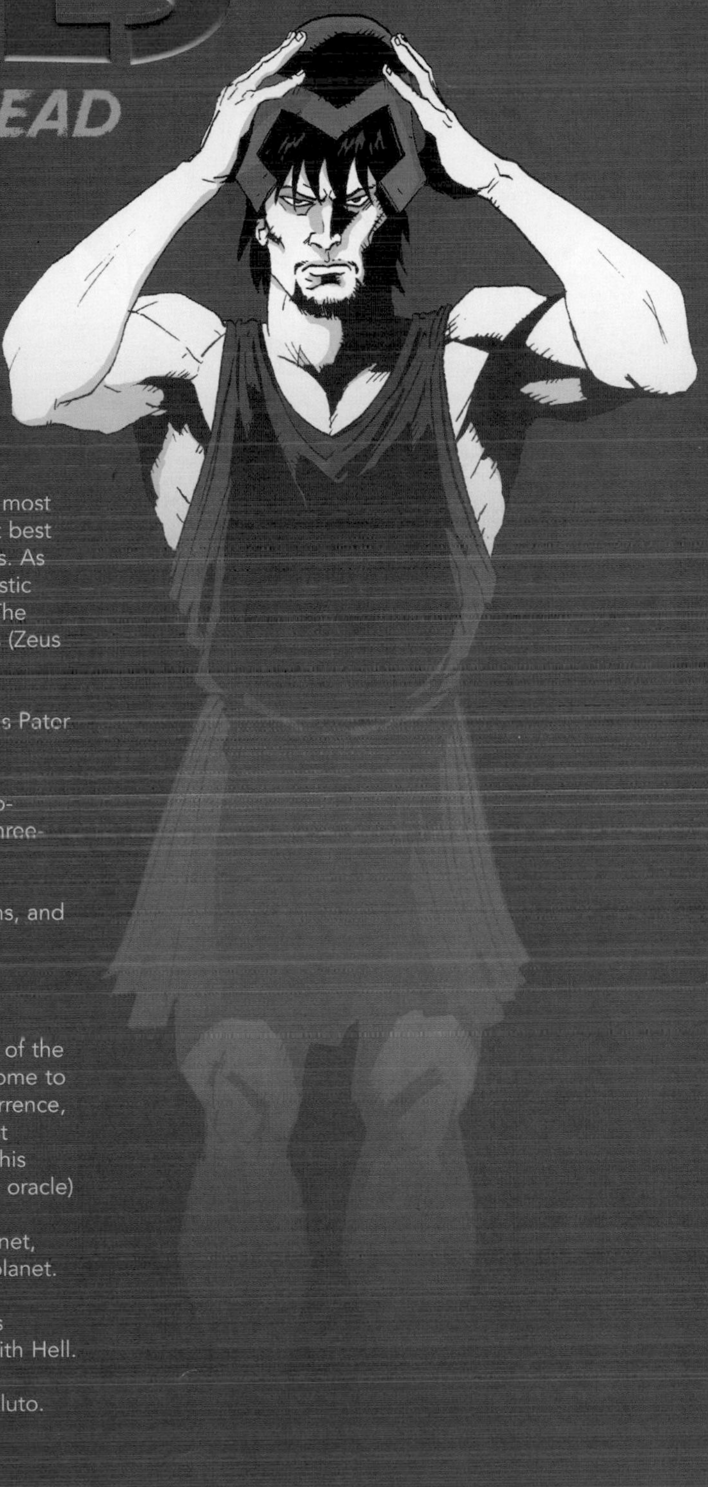

GOD OF Underworld, The Dead, Wealth

OTHER NAMES Though he was not an evil god, most ancient Greeks still considered it best to escape the attention of Hades. As a result they had many euphemistic names for him, such as Pluton (The Wealthy One) or Zeus Cythonios (Zeus of the Underworld)

ROMAN NAMES Pluto ("The Wealthy One") or Dis Pater ("The Rich Father")

SYMBOLS Helmet of Invisibility, Bident (two-pronged spear), Cerberus (the three-headed watchdog of Hades)

SARCRED ANIMALS Screech Owls, Black Sheep, Rams, and Cattle were sacrificed to him.

SACRED PLANTS Mint, Cypress, White Poplar

SACRED PLACES Hades; Elysium; Tartaros (realms of the dead in Ancient Greece); Elis (home to a temple to Hades—a rare occurrence, since, as mentioned above, most ancient Greeks wished to avoid his attention); Thesprotia (site of his oracle)

HEAVENLY BODY Pluto, formerly considered a planet, recently reclassified as a dwarf planet.

MODERN LEGACY The name Hades is still (perhaps unfairly) used interchangeably with Hell.

Mickey Mouse's dog is named Pluto. Maybe he's a very rich dog?

PERSEPHONE

DREAD QUEEN OF THE UNDERWORLD

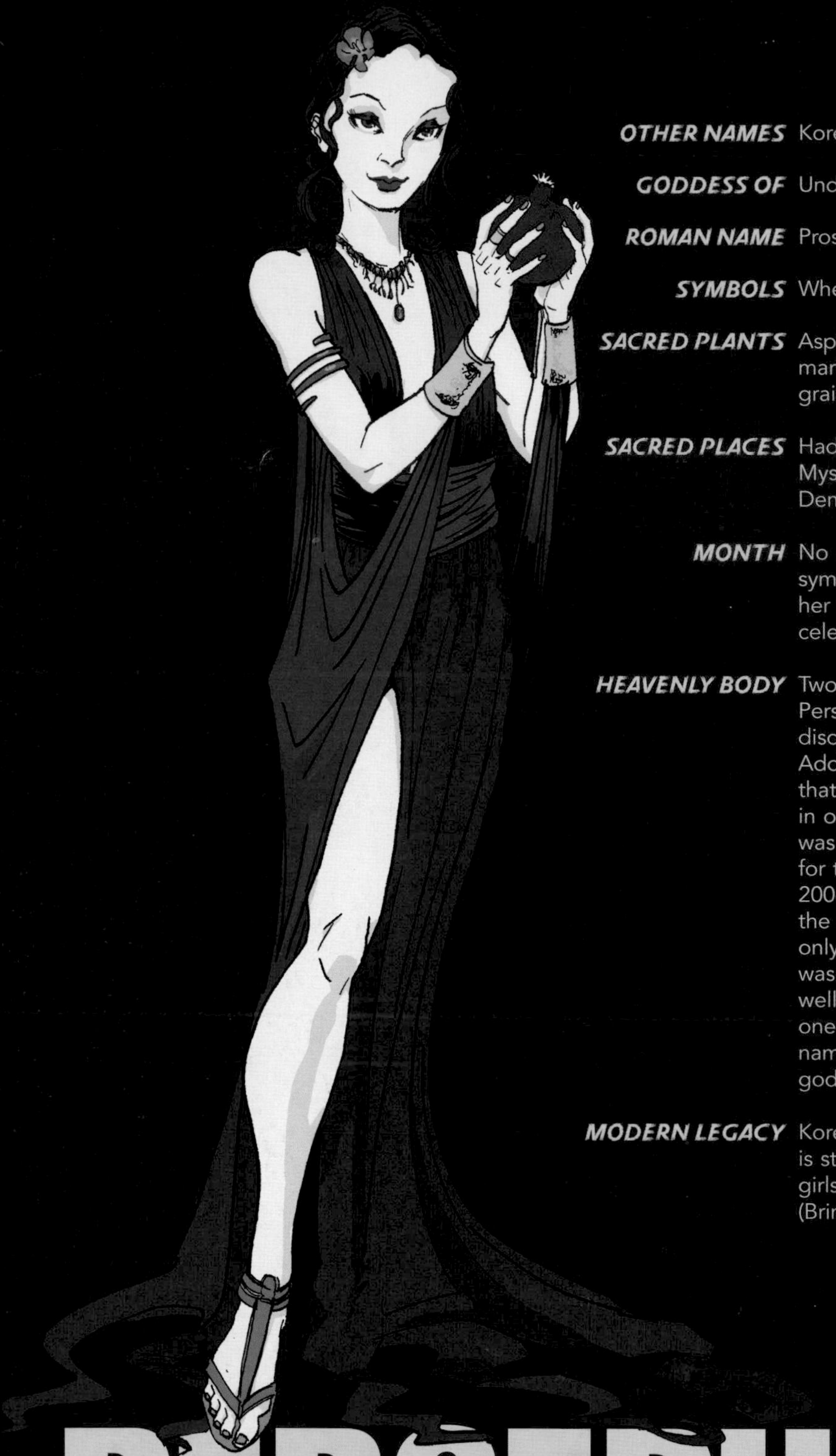

OTHER NAMES	Kore ("The Maiden")
GODDESS OF	Underworld, spring growth
ROMAN NAME	Proserpina
SYMBOLS	Wheat, Torch, Pomegranate
SACRED PLANTS	Asphodel, the plant of the dead; marigolds, crocuses, violets, seeds of grain
SACRED PLACES	Hades; Eleusis (site of the Eleusian Mysteries); any site where her mother, Demeter, was worshipped
MONTH	No one month in particular—as a symbol of the changing of the seasons, her return from the Underworld was celebrated in spring.
HEAVENLY BODY	Two, actually—an asteroid named Persephone and an even earlier-discovered asteroid named Proserpina. Additionally, in 2003, scientists thought that they had discovered a tenth planet, in orbit out beyond Pluto. Persephone was bandied about as a possible name for this heavenly body. However, in 2006, not only was it determined that the newly discovered tenth planet was only a dwarf planet, but the planet Pluto was also reclassified as a dwarf planet as well. Poor Persephone! Poor Hades! The one-time tenth planet has since been named (appropriately) Eris, after the goddess of discord.
MODERN LEGACY	Kore, more commonly spelled as Cora, is still a somewhat common name for girls. Her infernal name, Persephone (Bringer of Destruction), is less popular.

GⱤEEK NOTES

PAGE 2, PANEL 2: "Psychopompos," an epithet of Hermes', translates as "The Guide of Souls."

PAGE 3, PANEL 1: "Styx" translates as "gloomy" or "hated."

PAGE 4-5, PANEL 6: In case you didn't guess, that's Medusa the Gorgon. She ended up here after Perseus cut her head off in OLYMPIANS BOOK 2, ATHENA: GREY EYED GODDESS.

PAGE 4-5, PANEL 7: "The mortal half of Heracles"—this was a subject of much debate in the ancient world—did Heracles go to Hades when he died, like a mortal, or did he ascend to Olympus, like a god? I previously showed the latter in OLYMPIANS BOOK 3, HERA: THE GODDESS AND HER GLORY, and, indeed, there were many worshippers of Heracles that claimed he attained godhood upon his mortal demise. However, no less a source than the epic poem *The Odyssey* attests to Heracles being a denizen of Hades—Odysseus encounters Heracles (as well as Medusa) during his own visit to the Underworld. It was ultimately decided that, since Heracles was a demigod, his immortal half ascended to Olympus, while his mortal half descended to Hades. Bad luck to be Heracles' mortal half!

PAGE 6: The Titans were banished to Tartaros in OLYMPIANS BOOK 1, ZEUS: KING OF THE GODS, and the Hekatonchieres decided to stay on as their jailers in the same volume.

PAGE 7, PANEL 1: Ixion murdered his father-in-law by pushing him onto a bed of coals. Since he was the first murderer, I suppose no one really knew how to handle this sort of thing yet, so Zeus invited him to Olympus to explain himself. While there, rather than being grateful to the King of Gods, Ixion decided to try to assault Hera and got all blasted to bits by a lightning bolt for his troubles. Ixion—not a very smart guy.

PAGE 7, PANEL 2: Tityus is another big dummy. His punishment, of having his regenerating liver eaten by vultures, is a somewhat popular one. Watch future volumes of Olympians for the story of Prometheus, who suffers a similar fate.

PAGE 7, PANEL 3: The 49 husbands of the Danaides were the sons of Aegyptus, the king of Egypt. There were originally 50 of each—of the Danaides, only Hypermnestra decided not to kill her husband, Lynceus, and together they founded the royal family of Argos.

PAGE 7, PANEL 4: Another guy to watch future volumes of Olympians for. Occasionally you will see or hear the word "Sisyphean," which means "something that cannot be completed" and refers to this gentleman here.

PAGE 8: Asphodel is a type of flower believed to be the favorite food of the dead. "Lethe," appropriately enough, means "forgetfulness."

PAGE 10: Hades translates as "The Unseen One," a reference to his helmet of invisibility, given to him by the Cyclopes.

PAGE 11, PANEL 4: This line, "in the midst...men and gods" is directly quoted from the lost epic poem "The Titanomachy." Literally only a handful of lines survive, and this is one of them. I liked the idea of a dancing Zeus so much I made sure to fit it in here.

PAGE 13, PANEL 1: "Kore" translates as "The Maiden."

PAGE 14, PANEL 3: The song snippet that Apollo sings here and on the previous page is from "The Homeric Hymn to Demeter," one of the main texts I used as the basis for this book. It's too bad that Demeter gets rid of Apollo so quickly—she might have learned something had he continued the song. One wonders how Apollo might know a song that describes things that have not yet happened in this story, but, hey, he is the god of prophecy.

PAGE 17, PANEL 2: This new flower is a violet, for all you budding horticulturalists out there. The ancient sources actually name several different flowers for the scene here, but I liked this one the best.

PAGE 17, PANEL 8: Remember what I said about The Unseen One earlier?

PAGE 20, PANEL 2: The two-headed spear Hades has here is called a bident. It's like his brother Poseidon's three-headed spear, the trident. Tri, three, bi, two. Cool, huh?

PAGE 23, PANEL 4: The Lord of the Dead has a thing or two to learn about chivalry.

PAGE 27, PANEL 4: The sirens were creatures with the heads of beautiful women and the bodies of birds who used their magical singing voices to lure sailors to their doom in *The Odyssey* and other myths, and now you know how they got that way.

PAGE 31: From where does this new name "Persephone" come? Good question. It transliterates as "The Bringer of Destruction." Kind of an odd name for such a sweet girl, but then I guess she does have her dark side.

PAGE 33, PANEL 3: Regarding Tantalos's status as a favorite of the gods, in some sources he's considered a son of Zeus.

PAGE 33, PANEL 9: Ew. Poor Demeter...

PAGE 35, PANEL 2: Too little too late, Tantalos!

PAGE 35, PANEL 6: Pelops goes on to found one of the great ruling families of mythological Greece. The name Peloponnese, a region of modern day Greece, is derived from his name.

PAGE 37, PANEL 2: It does seem wasteful, doesn't it?

PAGE 37, PANELS 7, 8: If you cursed someone in the name the Furies, it was just about the worst thing that you could wish upon someone in ancient Greece. They were utterly tireless and remorseless, and would relentlessly hound whoever had been cursed.

PAGES 38, 39: Since Hades was god of the Underworld, which was underground, it was reasoned by the ancient Greeks that Hades was also the god of wealth, since precious stones and metals also came from underground.

PAGE 41: Hekate, "The Worker From Afar," is a very interesting mythological character, one whom I hope I will be able to explore further in future volumes. She was a goddess of the crossroads, magic, ghosts (all traits she shares with Hermes—note the Caduceus, his wand, in panel 5), and the night. She was often depicted in art as having three faces; the bottom row of panels is my little tip of the hat to that aspect of her.

PAGE 43, PANEL 5: This is a little joke by me, playing on the idea by some writers that the name Elysian is derived from an old Greek word meaning "lightning struck." It's funny, darnit! Laugh!

PAGE 44, PANEL 4: Hmmm...

PAGE 47, PANEL 2: Demeter is seen here carrying her Chrysaor, or Golden Blade.

PAGE 47, PANEL 5: I'll echo Hera here: Oh, Zeus...

PAGE 49: I showed this little interaction between Hekate and Hermes to spotlight the similarities in their functions, and also to show how they would probably like each other. Indeed, in some regions of Greece, it was believed that Hekate was Hermes' wife. Note also that I repeat the Hekate three-panel gag from page 41: I say, if something is funny the first time, it's funny every time (not true).

PAGE 50: This was a last minute addition to the story when I realized that we hadn't heard Hades' side of the story. I also wanted to put in a callback to the premonition of the Fates/Furies on page 37.

PAGE 51, PANEL 3: Askalaphos's not being very talkative is a reference to some versions of this story wherein Askalaphos rats out Persephone for eating the pomegranate seeds. Demeter is so enraged that she turns Askalaphos into a screech owl. It would seem that my version of Askalaphos has learned his lesson and just doesn't say very much at all.

PAGE 54, PANEL 1: As Kore renamed herself after she had been abducted, Hermes hasn't heard the name Persephone yet.

PAGE 57: See? I told you Persephone has a dark side. Nice assist from the god of lies, too. Incidentally, there is not a lot of agreement in the ancient sources on how many seeds Persephone ate, and how many months of each year she spent in the Underworld as a result. I went with six because I'm a big fan of duality.

PAGE 61, PANELS 5,6: Hermes' "special delivery" line here is a reference to his modern role as the emblem of the flower delivery service FTD. Persephone is the flower, naturally.

PAGE 63, PANEL 2: You can't say that Tanatalos didn't have this coming...

PAGE 65, PANEL 1: The three wise kings are Rhadymanthys, Minos, and Aiakos.

PAGE 66: Curiously, any myth that features the Underworld set after Persephone became the Queen of Hades also features Persephone—one would assume that at least 50 percent would take place while she was on Olympus; either that or a disproportionate number of myths are set during the winter months. More on this in my author's note.

ABOUT THIS BOOK

HADES: LORD OF THE DEAD is the fourth book in Olympians, a graphic novel series from First Second that retells the Greek myths.

FOR DISCUSSION

1 Hades is in love with Kore, so he kidnaps her and takes her to the Underworld. Is this an appropriate way to let someone know you like them? How could he have done it differently?

2 Which version of the Greek afterlife do you like better, the one described at the beginning, or Persephone's version?

3 The ancient Greeks considered it bad luck to say Hades' name, and instead came up with many titles for him, like The Wealthy One, or the Zeus of the Underworld. What would some other good labels for him be? How about the other gods?

4 If you were Persephone, would you rather stay with Hades or Demeter? How come?

5 In a lot of modern stories, people show Hades as a bad guy. Do you think Hades is a bad guy? How about Demeter? Was it fair that she turned Parthenope and Leukoesia into Sirens?

6 What on earth was Tantalos thinking when he cut up his son Pelops and tried to feed him to the Olympians? I mean, seriously?

7 Very few people believe in the Greek gods today. Why do you think it is important that we learn about them?

DEMETER

GOLDEN HAIRED

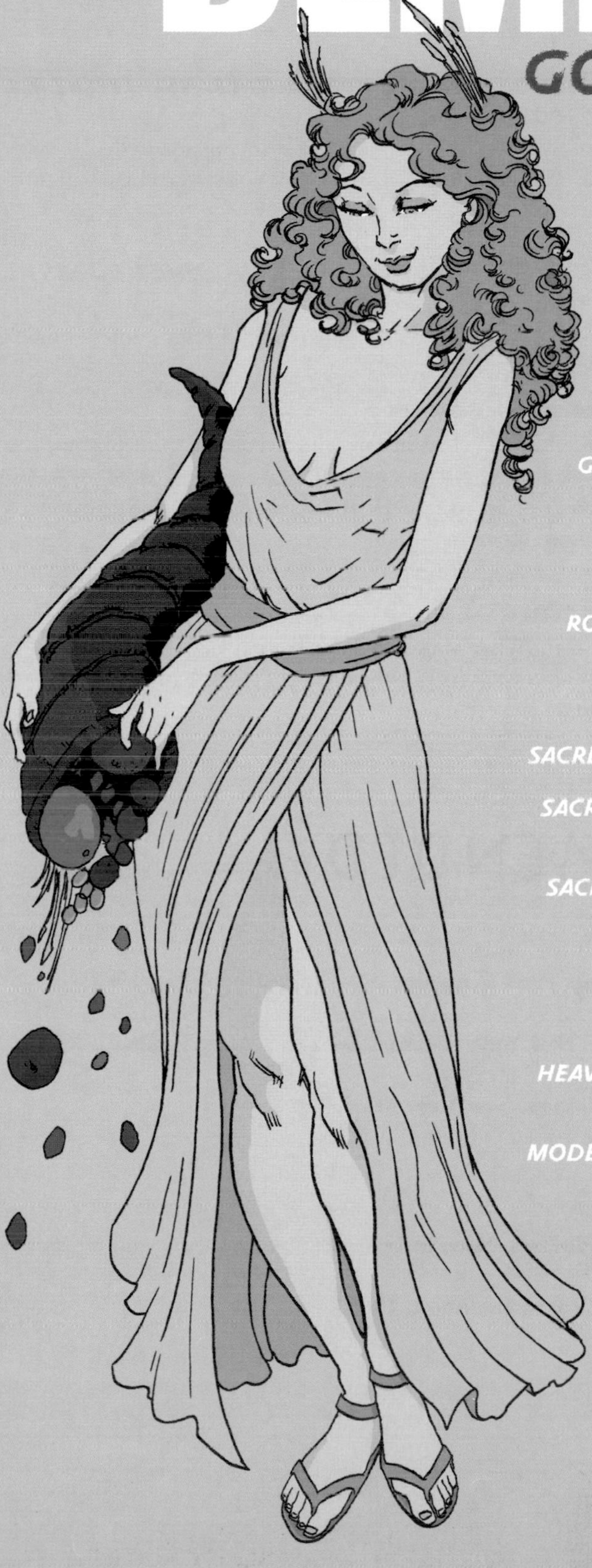

GODDESS OF Agriculture, grain, The Seasons, Fertile Soil, Bread. Also she was a principal goddess in the Mysteries, an offshoot of Oympian religion with a focus on a blessed afterlife.

ROMAN NAME Ceres

SYMBOLS Horn of Plenty (the cornucopia), Ear of Wheat, Torch, Golden Sword

SACRED ANIMALS Turtledove, Swine, Gecko

SACRED PLANTS Wheat, Barley, Grains, the Poppy, all cultivated crops

SACRED PLACES Eleusis (principal site of the Mysteries held in her honor), Sicily (site of her daughter Persephone's abduction by Hades)

MONTH August

HEAVENLY BODY Two of them: Ceres, a dwarf planet, and 1108 Demeter, an asteroid

MODERN LEGACY As befits the goddess of grain, we get the modern word "cereal" from Demeter's Roman name, Ceres.

BIBLIOGRAPHY

HOMERIC HYMNS. HOMERIC APOCRYPHA. LIVES OF HOMER. *EDITED AND TRANSLATED BY M.L. WEST. NEW YORK: LOEB CLASSICAL LIBRARY, 2003.*

As I mentioned elsewhere, the story of the abduction of Persephone is told in many, many myths by many, many authors. The *Homeric Hymn to Demeter* is one I used extensively for my version, and you can find it in this volume.

APOLLODORUS. *THE LIBRARY, EDITED AND TRANSLATED BY J.G. FRAZER, VOLUME 1: BOOKS 1-3.9 THEOGONY. NEW YORK: LOEB CLASSICAL LIBRARY, 1921.*

Another account of the abduction of Persephone is included in this volume, though I must confess I didn't utilize much from this telling.

THEOI GREEK MYTHOLOGY WEB SITE. WWW.THEOI.COM

Without a doubt, the single most valuable resource I came across in this entire venture. At theoi.com, you can find an encyclopedia of various gods and goddesses from Greek mythology, cross referenced with every mention of them they could find in literally hundreds of ancient Greek and Roman texts. Unfortunately, it's not quite complete, and it doesn't seem to be updated anymore.

MYTH INDEX WEB SITE WWW.MYTHINDEX.COM

Another mythology Web site connected to Theoi.com. While it doesn't have the painstakingly compiled quotations from ancient texts, it does offer some impressive encyclopedic entries of virtually every character to ever pass through a Greek myth. Pretty amazing.

ALSO RECOMMENDED
FOR YOUNGER READERS

D'Aulaires' Book of Greek Myths. Ingri and Edgar Parin D'Aulaire. New York: Doubleday, 1962.

Persephone. Sally Pomme Clayton and Virginia Lee. New York: Eerdmans Books for Young Readers, 2009.

Persephone the Phony. Joan Holub and Suzanne Williams. New York: Aladdin, 2010.

FOR OLDER READERS

The Marriage of Cadmus and Harmony. Robert Calasso. New York: Knopf, 1993.

Mythology. Edith Hamilton. New York: Grand Central Publishing, 1999.

Abandon. Meg Cabot. New York: Point, 2011.

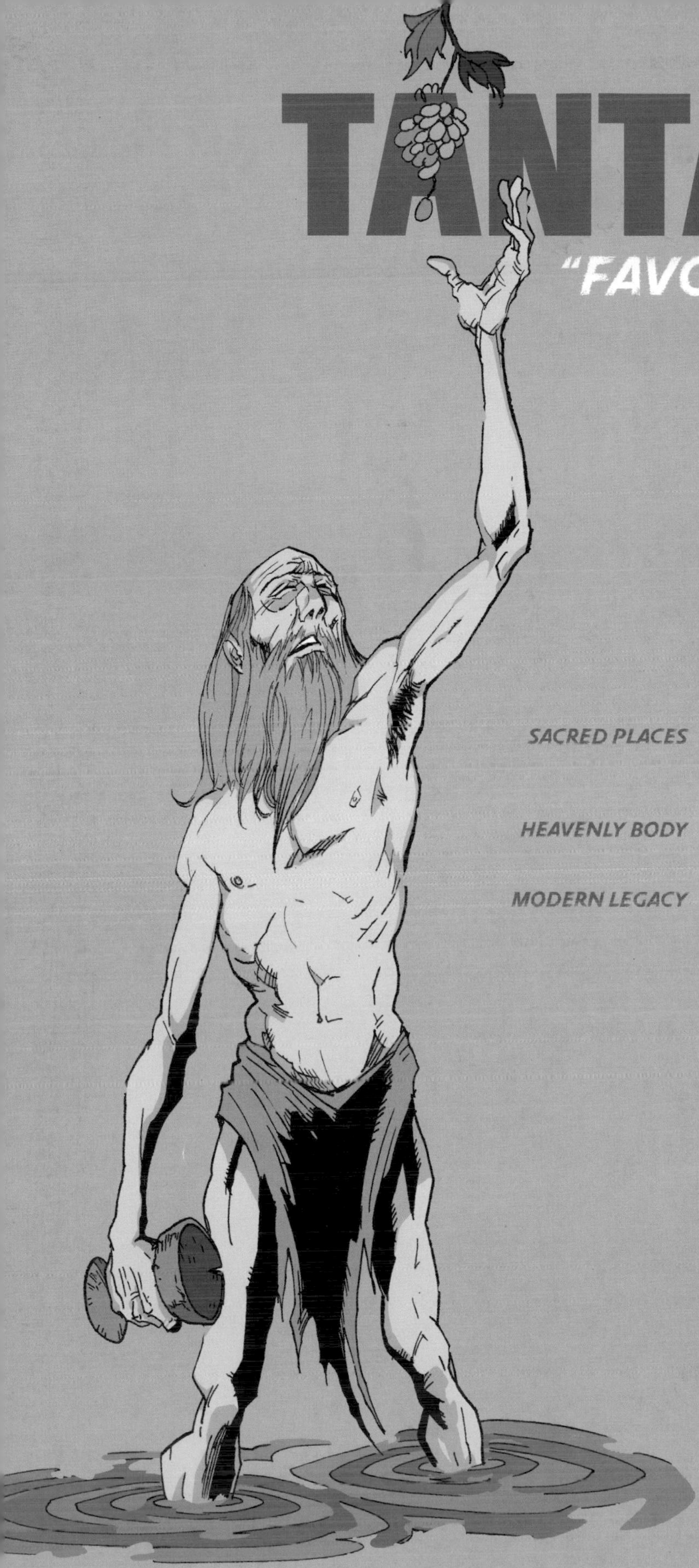

TANTALOS

"FAVORITE" OF ZEUS

SACRED PLACES Mount Sipylus in Turkey; the isle of Lesbos (site of shrines to him); Argos (his burial site)

HEAVENLY BODY There is a near-Earth asteroid named Tantalus

MODERN LEGACY Tantalos is the origin of the verb "tantalize," which means to tease or torment someone with something out of reach, or otherwise unobtainable.

A Tantalus is also a type of decanter, which has a clamp on the opening that prevents liquid from being poured out. Not too hard to figure out why they named it after Tantalos.

To everyone who's ever lived, loved, and died
– G.O.

First Second

New York & London

Copyright © 2012 by George O'Connor

A Neal Porter Book
Published by First Second
First Second is an imprint of Roaring Brook Press,
a division of Holtzbrinck Publishing Holdings Limited Partnership
175 Fifth Avenue, New York, New York 10010

Distributed in the United Kingdom by Macmillan Children's Books,
a division of Pan Macmillan.

Cataloging-in-Publication Data is on file at the Library of Congress

Paperback ISBN: 978-1-59643-434-9
Hardcover ISBN: 978-1-59643-761-6

First Second books are available for special promotions and premiums.
For details, contact: Director of Special Markets, Holtzbrinck Publishers.

First Edition 2012

Cover design by Mark Siegel and Colleen AF Venable
Book design by Colleen AF Venable and Danica Novgorodoff

Printed in August 2011 in China by Macmillan Production (Asia) Ltd.,
Kwun Tong, Kowloon, Hong Kong (supplier code 10)

Paperback: 10 9 8 7 6 5 4 3 2 1
Hardcover: 10 9 8 7 6 5 4 3 2 1

DATE DUE